FACE-Off

A Colorado Dragons Novel

D.M. DAVIS

FACE-Off by D.M. DAVIS
A part of The Colorado Dragons Series

eBook ASIN: B0GF6NMBMS
Paperback ISBN: 979-8-9869509-8-3

Published by D.M. DAVIS

www.dmckdavis.com
Cover Design by Thunderstruck Cover Designs
Cover Photo by Depositphotos
Editing by Tamara Mataya
Proofreading by Mountains Wanted Publishing & Indie Author Services
Formatting by Champagne Book Design

This story contains mature themes, strong language, and sexual situations. It is intended for adult readers. Some scenes may have triggers. See Content Warning page.

Human Authored™, Reg #: 6738140, https://authorsguild.org/human

ABOUT THIS BOOK

He's the team's captain—strong, empowering, and chivalrous.
She's a decorated veteran—smart, beautiful, and fierce.

I breathe, eat, and sleep hockey. It's my duty, my honor, my privilege to give all I have to my team, *for* my team. Lead by example. Leave the pain on the ice, wearing blood and sweat on my jersey with pride.

No sacrifice is too big… or so I thought.

Emmeline knows true sacrifice. Face of an angel. Heart of a warrior. Marine turned coffee shoppe owner, brewing a mean cup of joe kissed by the heavens, protective of her family by choice and those in need of saving.

I thought I knew sacrifice. I had no idea. Em makes me look like an amateur.

And I can't get enough. I can't get her out of my head, not that I want to.

But she's full up. She has no need nor desire for a pro athlete who lives in the limelight and dines with celebrities and politicians.

I face off with the toughest players in the NHL, yet I can't break the ice around her heart. I'm a warrior of a different kind, and I'm prepared to go to battle for her.

NOTE TO READER

I'm thankful to be writing in another shared world. I love the idea of each author penning their story from different perspectives of the characters who inhabit the Colorado Dragons' Universe. May your imagination run rampant and your soul soar on and off the ice with each book.

Creative license has been taken for the sake of the story, so please be gentle when reading the hockey scenes and details.

XOXO,
Dana
(D.M. DAVIS)

CONTENT WARNING

FACEOFF includes content that might not be suitable for some readers.

Sensitive Topics include: PTSD from military service, sexual assault (discussed but not on the page), domestic abuse (not the main characters), codependency.

Please read responsibly.

DEDICATION

For the warrior in all of us. May we find a safe place to rest and a warm body to remind us we don't always have to be strong to be loved.

FACE-
Off

CHAPTER 1

NIGHTLY

ORGANIZED CHAOS IS THE ONLY WAY TO DESCRIBE it. Lotti's Latte is packed and smells like a rich roast I just want to nuzzle, breathe in, and take a moment—or two—with. When Carol, our owner's assistant, recommended the coffee here, I figured it'd be just like any other coffee house. But I didn't expect this, especially not at 6:45 in the morning.

The volume of chattering discontent is loud enough to rattle my not-quite-awake brain, making me wish I was still in bed and not standing in line for the hot pick-me-up my caffeine-depleted body desperately needs. If I don't get it in the next ten minutes, I'll be late for practice. Which will only piss off Coach, and no one wants that, especially me. I'm one of his faves, but there's no reason to test his patience.

I lean toward the guy next to me, eyeing the employee behind the register who is beyond flustered and on the verge of tears. "What's going on?"

On a long sigh, he turns his scowl on me before his brows jump when he looks up, and up, to meet my questioning gaze. "Damn."

Yeah, I get that a lot. I'm big. Move on. I let my own quirked brow restate my question. *What the fuck's going on?*

"Oh, um, the espresso machine is broken, but Em promises it'll be fixed lickety-split."

"Em?" I cock my head, perusing the jumble of baristas behind the counter where he gestured.

"Emmeline. The owner." He points to the dark-haired beauty who swiftly enters from the back, fully on a mission.

"Ah." Good to know, I guess. I came for a coffee, not a history lesson on who runs this joint.

Before I can ask if he knows how long "lickety-split" equates to, the owner, Em, gracefully leaps onto the counter and whistles like she's a ref at one of my games, except she uses two fingers in her mouth instead of an actual whistle, instantly quieting the crowd. The sound reverberates in my ears long after she stops. Impressive. Damn, she may be one intriguing history lesson.

After raising her hands, getting most everyone's attention like the Pied Piper of coffee she apparently is, she wipes her brow with the towel she plucks from her apron. "Folks, I'm sorry for the delay. The espresso machine is fixed, and we'll get you your beverages as soon as humanly possible. Those of you *waiting* for your order, please move over to the left." She points to the PICK-UP sign hanging from the ceiling. "Those waiting to *place* your order," she taps the ORDER HERE sign above her head, "we're open for business again."

Before she moves to get down, a big guy steps up behind her and lifts her off the counter with a firm grip around her waist, easing her down, ensuring she's steady on her own two feet. She scowls at him and grumbles, "Was that necessary?"

"Yes." He bops her nose, completely ignoring her displeasure.

His hand lingers on her hip for just a moment before he dives into the fray of fulfilling orders.

Unease washes over me as my gut twists at their interplay. They're obviously close, but how close? Are they together?

Not that it matters.

Not that I'm *looking*.

It's just… to have someone to watch after like he obviously does, to care for her, to be so at ease to simply snatch her off the counter before any potential harm could come to her. She didn't seem to need his help, but still he was there, watchful, protective. Her rock.

I want that.

Yearning pings in the dead space in my chest I've long since given up trying to fill. It's an echo of a dream that barely has a spark left, but still, it's enough to rouse my desire for a woman of my own to cherish, protect, ignite.

My world doesn't leave much space for genuine connections. It's all puck-bunnies and wannabees who want to fuck me or fuck someone I introduce them to. I love what I do. I don't love the tarnished world pro-athlete fame has dropped me into.

I am blessed in so many ways, but not in the ways of love, of having a life partner to walk through the good and the bad with, to rest my weary soul with on lazy Sunday mornings, cuddling through the cold-ass winter, hiking the wilderness in spring, surfing the summer away, and baking through fall.

Ah, fuck, the dream is good and alive, and its face, in the form of Emmeline—the owner with dark, silken hair unfairly bound from view on top her head and golden eyes that pierce my soul—staring right at me, about to take my order, and I'm worried what will fly out of my mouth is, *You. I'll have you.*

EMMELINE

Skirting around Marcus at the register, I get the attention of Mr. Tall, Dark, and Gorgeous with a double-click of my tongue as if I'm asking a horse to gallop, or better yet, maybe I'm asking him for a ride. "What can I get you, handsome?" I'd call him beautiful if I didn't think I'd offend his sensibilities. But damn, he is a beautiful specimen of a man I wouldn't mind riding for an hour or two. Maybe more. I don't do commitment. But I'd totally *do* him.

I throw in a wink as his gaze meets mine, might as well get this ball rolling. Momma has work to do and a tall drink of water—er, tree—to climb.

His scowl is torturously sexy with a hint of warning, as though he doesn't suffer fools lightly, and yet, I'm drawn to him. Maybe I wasn't born with the gene to find *him* scary. "Did you just *click* your tongue at me and call me *handsome*?"

The lower octave of his voice resonates in my belly, curling the corner of my mouth into a crooked smile. "Maybe. Now, what can I get you?" I glance behind him with some relief to find the line has shortened dramatically. My team is doing their job of taking orders and kicking butt to fulfill them. "I'm sure an important man like you has somewhere to be." Like in my pants, but I'm not that crass or needy. Okay, maybe needy, but not crass enough to say it.

His stare is intense, but the tenderness in his eyes has my heart fluttering for reasons I will undoubtably analyze in great detail later.

"I'd like a caffè Americano with vanilla, a dark hazelnut Americano, two iced lattes—all large; and four cinnamon scones, two apple and two cherry turnovers." He glances at the menu. "Oh, and a bacon, egg, and cheese croissant with a bottled water, and... make that two caffè Americano with vanilla." His blue eyes lock with mine. "Please." He holds out a hundred-dollar bill. "Keep the change."

Keep the change, I repeat in my head along with his order. He must be hungry. "Name?"

"Night—" He stutters to a stop.

"Knight?" Just Knight, as in "knight in shining armor"? Is he a good guy looking to save fair maidens?

I swear he blushes as he clears his throat. "Nightly. My friends call me Nightly."

I start to write his *name,* K-N-I-G-H-T-L-Y.

He leans in, pointing to my order pad. "No K, just N-I-G-H-T-L-Y. I'm no knight—"

"—in shining armor?" I smirk up at his substantial size hovering over the counter.

His blush only deepens as he shakes his head. Hmm, I'm not convinced. But Nightly? I'd do him nightly. Someone's got to be a lucky girl to have him service her needs *nightly*. Maybe I could be that woman for a night or two. I mark out the K on my order pad and hand it, along with his hundred-dollar bill, to Marcus to ring up.

Marcus eyes the bill and me. We don't usually take large currency. I simply nod and direct Mr. Big Bucks to the pick-up counter. "Your order will be ready in a minute, Mr. Nightly."

"Just Nightly."

Right. "Mr. Just Nightly," I tease as I get to work on his order. Man must be hungry *and* thirsty, though I'm certain he's taking this to the office or something. I eye his jeans, t-shirt, and brown leather jacket—not typical office attire. But this is Colorado. Not all businessmen wear suits.

I package up *Nightly's* food while Suze tackles his drinks. I throw in an extra croissant, not just because he paid extra. Based on his muscles bulging under his jacket, he needs a lot of fuel. I slip my business card with my name, cell, and a quick note into his bag before I can chicken out. I'm no scaredy-cat.

Once ready, I carton up his drinks and slide them across the counter along with the cute brown twine-handled paper bag featuring the Lotti's Latte logo, with plenty of napkins tucked inside to keep the food warm. "Sorry for the chaos today. I hope you enjoy your drinks and food." And *come back anytime*. I hold back the cheesy comment.

My confidence only goes so far when it comes to hot guys. Plus, if he noticed my flirting, he's not biting, which only makes me regret the note I left in his bag. Desperate much? *Don't be so needy, Em.*

His gaze flashes to my mouth. "If it tastes half as good as it looks and smells, I'm certain I'll be back for more."

Yes. Please. My foolish heart leaps. "Soon then." I wink before turning to find Bennett's eyes on us with a raised brow and a knowing smile. "Shut up," I whisper as I escape to my office to regroup.

I'm normally not such a desperate horndog. What's wrong with me? Oh, that's right, Mr. Tall, Dark, and Gorgeous hit me with a pheromone bomb, and my ovaries are dancing for the pretty man, flagging him in. Hussies, both of them.

CHAPTER 2

NIGHTLY

I'M BOTH SLUGGISH FROM THE SUGAR AND HYPED from all the caffeine I drank before practice. One of the caffè Americano with vanilla was for me, but I felt like a hoarder wanting to keep all her goodies for myself. I finally relented and shared, but only after they granted me a taste. I don't know if Emmeline Weston is a witch or just that talented, but everything was decadent and delicious. Even now, hours later, the memory of her negotiating the chaos of her shoppe and the taste of her goodies only makes me crave more of her life-affirming coffee and the woman herself.

Her business card, sitting on my desk with her note to *call her for a ride sometime,* taunts me.

I'm not certain, but by *ride,* I believe she means riding my dick or me riding her. Her boldness takes me by surprise. Not a turn-off, not completely, but a surprise all the same. She was flirty, but that could be her nature or a tactic to keep customers coming back.

I've been approached by emboldened women before. Early in my career, I loved it. Saw it as a compliment that they felt secure in themselves to take charge of their sexuality. Now, it feels more like taking a piece of me for themselves. The overly sexual overtures say more about them than me. I'm just a notch on their bedpost, the trinket on the hood of their car, a hot sweaty moment they'll get off to sometime in the future. They undoubtedly see me as a conquest to further their agenda, their ego, their fantasies. It has nothing to do with me, Carter McNight, and everything to do with them.

Hence, the empty hollow space in my chest that never gets filled. I'm not looking for meaningless sexual encounters. Not anymore, not in a long while. I want a woman who respects me and herself enough to ask for more, expect more. Expect the romance, the wining and dining, the dating, the flirting, the tease of secret kisses and heated glances. The idea of finding that, gets my dick hard.

Though, for a brief moment, a quick tangle with Emmeline is appealing, in the end, she deserves more. *I* deserve more.

I toss her card in a drawer, hiding it from sight, from temptation.

If I *want* more, I'm going to have to *be* more.

EMMELINE

I can't get Mr. Tall, Dark, and Gorgeous out of my head. I couldn't help but notice his rather hulking form waiting to place his order, checking the time on his sizable watch instead of his phone, which was nowhere to be seen. I had to look away before anyone noticed my drooling and return to my task of helping clear the backorders. My patrons are patient on a good day, but on a screwy day like today, I'm pressing my luck expecting them to wait as long as they did, much less hope they come back to find today was not the norm. My shop runs smoothly, like the well-oiled machine it is.

Only, not today.

"What do you mean you don't know what I'm referring to?" A tight glance with clenched jaw is all I get before Bennett returns his focus to the pot where he sautés the holy trinity for the gumbo he insisted on making.

Not that he has to twist my arm to cook whatever his big heart desires. He's one heck of a chef. He missed his calling, or maybe he's found it.

Years in the Marines, like us, can lead a person to find new ways to comfort the restlessness of our souls after leaving active duty. He found cooking. I found my mom's coffee shoppe and baking. Though, to be honest, it was thrust upon me, but now I'm thankful all the same. After a long day of disaster after disaster, I'm more than happy to let him pamper me with a homecooked meal.

Today was a total nightmare of delayed deliveries and a repairman who didn't show, forcing us to delve into the innards of a machine I know how to work blindfolded with one arm behind my back, but I don't know diddly about its inner workings. Luckily, Bennett is a whiz with all things food *and* mechanical. He didn't even want me to call the repair guy. I insisted, touting we pay for the service for a reason. It's a waste of money if Benny does all the work. "Exactly," was his only response.

If I let him, he'd be my handyman one hundred percent of the time. I can't take advantage of him like that. He saved my life by coming with me to Colorado to run my mom's coffee shoppe when she was sick. He stuck with me through her illness, her passing, mounds of paperwork and tax law, coming out the other side to revitalize Lotti's Latte in her honor. He's my best friend and manager. I can't ask him to wear the repair-guy hat too.

He clears his throat. "Earth to space cadet."

He forces my smile by simply being him, my bestie. "I mean, dear Benny—"

"Don't call me that."

"—we served a lot of customers today, and I'm sure many of them were quite attractive."

"Like you don't know exactly who I'm referring to. The giant in the leather jacket, jeans, and work boots like he's any ole dude coming in for coffee before hitting the construction site instead of heading to the rink for practice."

My head shoots up. "What?! Rink? Practice?" I nearly slice my finger deveining a shrimp. I rinse it and my hands off before turning to fully face my best friend. "Explain." No more pretenses I don't know who he's giving me the third degree over.

"Nightly? Ring any bells, darlin'?"

Frowning, I mull over why that name sounds so familiar. Wait! He said rink. "You mean…" Holy mother… "Are you saying I propositioned Carter McNight? The Colorado Dragons' center?"

Bennett's smile irritates my shock as he boops my nose. "One and the same, baby doll. One and the same."

"No…" Heat creeps up my chest to my neck, taking root as a full-on flush. "No. No. No. No. No. I did not hit on one of the most eligible womanizers in the NHL." *Please tell me you invented a time machine so I can go back to this morning and "undo" that wretched note. Please, Doc Brown, lead me to your DeLorean.*

"Firstly, he's not a womanizer, at least not anymore."

"Right, because you know him so well."

"Secondly, how exactly did you proposition him, my dear Aphrodite?"

I resume cleaning the shrimp, no longer desiring eye contact for this discussion. "I may have slipped a note in with his food."

Mortification rings anew. "He probably didn't even see it and tossed it out with the bag."

"Or"—my irritatingly honest best friend enjoys rubbing my nose in my mistake—"he's sitting, wherever hockey stars relax—"

"In a bar with a puck bunny on his lap." Grinding her pleasure into him or out of him, depending on how you look at it. Either way, this is the *true* disaster of my day.

"I'm telling you, he doesn't do that kind of stuff anymore. He's probably at home alone or with a few teammates having a beer and watching Sports Center, contemplating your remarkably enticing offer *of*...?"

Nope. No way am I repeating those words. *Oh. My. God. THOSE words. Crass. I was so crass and... mediocre.* How many times does he get hit on in a day? I'm sure I'm one of dozens—no wonder he didn't flirt back. "It doesn't matter. He'll never come in the shop again. So, let's drop it." *Please. I'm begging you to drop it.*

"Mmhmm." He dumps more ingredients into the large stock pot. "Tell me what you wrote, and I'll drop it."

"No." Nope. Not happening.

"You offered to service his dragon?" he suggests oh so helpfully, completely delighted with himself.

I shake my head. "Not saying."

"No, you didn't recognize him, which"—he points at me—"I'm sure he found endearing."

"The man gets hit on all the time. I doubt anything I did or said was a blip on his radar." *Please, God, let the man have forgotten about me and... AND thrown away Lotte's Latte bag without him or any of the other players seeing my business card. Amen and thank you.*

I can picture them now, having a grand ole laugh at my expense. The poor coffee shoppe girl desperately offering the famous athlete a *ride*. Gah, kill me now.

"I saw the way he was looking at you. You are way more than a blip in his day. You are a delicious morsel he wants to taste over and over again."

Jesus, it is hot in here? I take a long drink of water. Why is this man my best friend? "Why are you so mean?"

He chuckles, full-on belly laughs. "Ah, baby doll, it's called ribbing. I know your skin is thicker than this."

I'm a duck. Water off my back.

"But then again, you always let me see your sweet side." His voice softens, gentles, reminding me *why* he's my best friend. We've saved each other's lives more times than either of us can remember. He's earned his place at my side because of what he's done, who he is with me, what he'll do to protect what's his. *I'm* his.

He's mine.

The. End.

"I said, 'Call me for a ride sometime,'" I murmur, holding his tender gaze.

"Em," he sighs.

"I know." I blink back ridiculous tears. I haven't cried since my mom died. Well, and possibly the months that followed. I don't cry, and I don't desperately hit on strangers who are actually NHL pro athletes who have no place for a woman like me in their lives. I'm complicated. I have big, heavy, burdensome baggage, and though Nightly looks strong enough, my baggage comes with landmines and booby-traps.

Besides, he's famous. I don't do famous.

"He'll call." Bennett kisses my check and goes back to his gumbo pot.

"He won't," I pray.

Sadly, he doesn't.

CHAPTER 3

EMMELINE

DAYS, A WEEK, TWO WEEKS GO BY WITH NO SIGN OF Carter McNight, besides on TV. We've suddenly become dedicated Dragons fans who watch every game and root for him to score from the safety of my home or Bennett's, which is basically the same since Bennett lives next door. It's weird. I'd barely met Nightly, and now I'm a fan wishing him well at every turn and hoping to see him back in my store nearly as much as I hope to never see him again.

I'm a conundrum. Never tried or claimed to be any different. Take me or leave me; it's not going to change who I am.

A raised voice garners my attention. As I scoop ice for an iced coffee, I catch Tish wiping at the corner of her eyes as the man across from her berates her with hands flying and his voice getting louder. I hand the cup to Suze. "I'll be right back."

Circling the counter, I grab a few muffins, noting Bennett's, "Careful, Em."

Stopping at the table by the window, I paste on an easy smile. *Kill 'em with kindness* is the motto of the moment. "Hi, Tish." I set the muffins on a napkin at their table.

"Emmeline," she exhales, dutifully swiping at her face, glancing at the man across from her.

"Thought you might like some muffins. Be sure you have some food in your stomach before you head to work."

"Thanks. That's—"

Facing the angry gentleman, I offer him a chance to cool off before things get too heated. "What can I get you to drink?"

"Nothing," he grumbles.

"You sure? It's on the house. Not even some water?" I catch his gaze and hope he sees more than a friendly-face façade that can change at a drop of a hat, a cruel word, or a raised fist.

"Sure, whatever," he brushes me off.

"Great." I wave at my bestie behind the counter. "Hey, Bennett, toss me a water, would ya?"

Bennett, ever the eagle-eye, keeps his focus on me as he throws a bottled water over other customers' heads. With barely a glance, I snatch it out of the air and set it in front of mister. "Here ya go." I catch Tish's gaze. "Let me know if I can get you anything else."

"We were just leaving," the man rasps, standing and nearly knocking over his chair before I catch it.

"I'm not leaving just yet," Tish says softly, eyes on the banana-nut muffin she's tearing apart more than eating.

"No rush on my account." I pick up his water. "Don't forget this. Would you like a bag for your muffin?" I practically shove both into his hands, keeping them occupied and his focus on me.

"Nah." He glances at Tish, then me, back to her. "I… ugh… see you later." He turns, leaving without a reply, seemingly more defeated than angry.

I don't take my eyes off him as he exits and disappears out of sight. The tension eases, but I don't count us in the clear, not yet.

"I'm sorry," Tish's whisper draws me back to her.

"No need to apologize. You weren't the one making a scene." That was all Jimmy. It's not his first time, but I hope it's the last. I squeeze her shoulder. "You want to come to the back, take a minute?"

She's shaking her head before I even finish my offer. "No, I'm just going to finish my coffee and muffin. Then I'll get out of your hair."

"As I said, don't rush off on my account." I lean down until we lock eyes and offer, "You need me to walk you to work, you say the word. Me or Bennett, we'd be happy to."

As I say his name, a warm hand presses to my back. "Tish, you let me know when you're ready, and it'll be my pleasure to escort you to work. It's been a minute since I've seen May, gives me a good reason to drop in."

Tish works at a vet's office a few blocks away with Bennett's cousin May.

"You sure?" The uncertainty in her voice rolls in my stomach. Tish has been coming here for years, before my mom passed. Bennett's connection got her the receptionist job at Dr. Werner's veterinary clinic. Now, she's working toward being a vet tech like May.

"Of course I'm sure, darlin'. You enjoy your breakfast." He slips a water and a foil-wrapped egg, sausage, and cheese bagel in front of her. "Eat. I'll be ready when you are."

Her teary gaze meets ours. "Thank you both. You've no idea..." her voice cracks, snatching her next words.

I swipe at her stream of tears and hand her more napkins from the stash in my apron. "Family watches out for each other, Tish. You're a part of Lotti's, the reason we're still around after my mother passed. Your loyalty kept us going even when Bennett and I didn't know what we were doing."

"Your mom started a great thing, but you two have brought it a new life." She looks around the warm décor, with a newly added fireplace and revamped living-room type seating for those who don't want to sit at a table. "It's so homey in here now. I never want to leave."

Bennett chuckles, offering her his award-winning smile. "And no one is asking you to." He raps the table with his knuckles. "Holler when you're ready."

Then he pulls me away with his large arm around my back, an arm that's always safe, never threatening. Despite his size, he's a teddy bear to me but a grizzly to others when needed. Leaning in close as we turn, he whispers, "He's here."

NIGHTLY

It riles me, the way his hands seem at home on her body. Are they lovers? Exes? Friends with benefits? I've been captivated since entering Lotti's, catching her zip around the counter, food in hand, getting right in the face of the couple having a heated discussion. Well, his side was heated. I'm not sure the woman actually said anything until Emmeline arrived at their table like a godsend, based on the relief on the woman's face.

I'm not sure what would have happened if Emmeline didn't insert herself into their interaction. It didn't look like anything good. I haven't been here long enough to witness its escalation. I only caught a few rough words before she jumped into action, with Bennett's focus solely on her, ready to provide backup if needed. But she didn't need it. She handled that guy like a pro. She'd make a good ref or a cop with her ability to deescalate potentially volatile situations.

Spinning her around, Bennett motions to me. I didn't even realize he'd noticed my arrival in all the commotion. If she's shocked to see me—or hell, even happy—she hides it well. The tenderness she showed her customer is replaced by a business-friendly smile as she offers a swift "hello" and a nod as she passes, disappearing behind the counter.

That's it? That's all I get?

It's been weeks of holding back, waiting until I couldn't stand it a second more, memorizing each stroke of her handwritten note on her business card until I'm certain I could duplicate it in my sleep. Not that I intend to take her up on her offer, or not *just* her offer.

She's clearly an independent, self-reliant woman who doesn't need a man to make her way in the world easier. She's forged her own path—or maybe he's forged it with her. He's protective. He cares—that's obvious to anyone witnessing their interactions. She scowls at him, and his smile only grows. Whatever they have—it runs deep. Maybe he's fulfilling a need in her life where she's not open to anyone new? Hence, the cold shoulder.

Wait, but *she* propositioned me.

Bennett sidles up to next me, his gaze following her as she fills orders behind the counter. "You're going to have to work harder than that if you want to win her over."

"I've gathered. I thought after the note..." Shit, maybe he doesn't know about the note.

"She'd be easy?" He side-eyes me.

"No. Not easy." I shake my head, chuckling, "More... approachable."

"Mmm, yeah, no." His knowing smile is irritating and gives me pause.

"I'm not sure if you're trying to help me or scare me off." I catch

Emmeline glaring at us. She's certainly leaning toward the *scare me off* option.

"Let's call it an assist. I can get you closer to the goal, but I can't help you score. That's all you." He crosses his arms, leaning into the wall, happy with his sports analogy.

"Still not sure if you're helping me."

With a nod to the woman in question, he claims, "I'm helping *her*," and slips behind the counter.

CHAPTER 4

NIGHTLY

I STAND LIKE A SAP, CONTEMPLATING MY NEXT MOVE. Maybe there is no *next* move. If she's not interested, what's the point? But *she* flirted with me and put that note in my bag. She may be having second thoughts, but the attraction is there, I'm sure of it. I knew I'd have to work at it if I wanted more than a wham-bam-thank-you-ma'am encounter.

Let's get to work proving myself to her. I'm worth getting to know. *She's* worth more than a quick fuck.

Bennett eyes me over the counter, nodding to the spot beside him where Emmeline has her back to me, working on an order, doing pretty much anything to avoid me, it feels like. I nod and move to the register. Bennett whispers something that has her turning, our eyes locking, and I swear I can hear her breath quicken and heart pound at a rate that equals my own.

Swiping her hands on her apron, she approaches, whipping her dark ponytail over her shoulder. "Have you been helped?"

I want to laugh. This woman, she knows I haven't been helped. "No," I simply reply.

"Oh, sorry about that." She doesn't seem sorry at all. "What can I get you?"

"Two things."

"Okaaay." She waits expectantly.

"A large dark hazelnut Americano."

She smiles, as if she remembers my order from weeks ago, though that time, I had it with vanilla. Two of them. I'm still jittery from the memory. "What else?" she prompts.

"I'd like a moment to speak with you, perhaps outside, or in your office?" Any place where I'm not speaking to her with a counter between us, where I feel like my only importance is as a customer. Somewhere without an audience. My life is enough of a spectacle. I don't need witnesses if she turns me down.

Contemplating, she glances around, then back to me. "Okay, let me get your coffee first." She turns, leaving me at the counter, not even ringing me up so I can pay.

I drop a twenty in the tip jar and catch Bennett beaming at me. I shake my head, not sure how to read the situation. She agreed too easily. Maybe she thinks I have a business deal for Lotti's or something. Her giving me a chance is not a sure thing.

Yet, Bennett seems entirely too happy about our interaction. Maybe he is on my side a little bit. Or more like, he's on my side if he thinks I'm good for her. I can be. I *hope* to be. If she has any inspiration to find more in life, I'd like a chance at being her *more*.

Within minutes, she's at my side handing me my drink. "We can step outside."

I move to follow, barely making it in time to reach over her head to push the door open. She frowns as she passes, as though she doesn't like the door being held for her. I'll work on that. Baby steps. I have to get her to talk to me first, or better yet, agree to go out with me.

With a soft touch on her lower back, I guide us farther from the entrance of her shoppe, near the parking lot where no one will hear our conversation. Nerves spike, rattling my confidence. I practically shove my drink at her. "Would you like a sip?" She should have the first taste. She may not be into sharing, but I definitely don't mind drinking after her.

"Uh," she scowls at my coffee but takes it, "suuure." She watches me as I watch her take a tentative taste and then a deeper pull, a faint smile touching the corner of her lips.

"Good, huh?" I ordered the caffè Americano with vanilla last time, but I think this is my new favorite based on the sample I had of the one I gave away a few weeks ago… *and* the fact she's thoroughly enjoying it now.

"Yeah, it's my favorite." She's just cementing my selection further.

"For good reason," I reply. She moves to hand it back to me, but I stop her. "You drink it. I'll get another for the road." I only have a few minutes before I need to leave for practice. I should have waited to come until tomorrow, when I had an off morning, but I couldn't wait another hour, much less another day.

"You sure?" She takes another swallow before I even answer.

I don't hide my smile. "Positive. You're enjoying it too much for me to take it from you." Like taking candy from a baby, who would do that? Not me.

"That's… thanks." After another indulgent mouthful, she catches my gaze. "What did you want to talk about?"

Awkwardness creeping back in, I run my hand along the back of my neck before catching myself. "I'd normally ask you out for coffee, something simple, small, but given you own your own coffee shoppe, what would you say to dinner… or lunch if you prefer?"

"I'd say I don't know you." The sharpness is back in her tone.

"You're right." I hold out my hand. "I'm Carter McNight. I'm a decent guy. Though, I guess if I were an ass, I wouldn't admit I was… only *I* would." I shrug. "I tend to be more honest than some people care for."

"I like honest. It's better than the alternative." She tosses her empty cup in the trash a few feet away.

"Agreed. So, I promise to always be honest with you whether you say yes or no."

She nods, considering as she shakes my hand. "I'm Emmeline Weston, owner of Lotti's. You've met Bennett, my manager and best friend—"

"Not officially." Though I feel like I know him already from the brief interaction earlier.

"Then I'll introduce you."

Noting the best friend status, I have a feeling he's going to be very important in my ability to woo this woman. "It's nice to officially meet you, Emmeline."

"Same." Her attention is drawn down the sidewalk, toward her shop. "It's Em, if you like." She rocks back, taking one step then another. "I've gotta—" Before she finishes, she's off like a rocket, running the way we came.

Glancing to the front of her shoppe, I catch sight of the same couple who were arguing earlier—the man apparently not happy with the outcome—decided to come back to finish their disagreement.

Only, he's no longer talking.

Arm raised, he strikes the woman across the face seconds before Emmeline reaches them.

EMMELINE

Son of a bitch, I roar internally. Seconds after Tish's boyfriend strikes her, I'm there, locking him in a chokehold, kicking his knees out from under him with one arm behind his back, forcing the asshole to the ground. "Stay down, asshole," I growl in his ear as he fights to gain the upper hand.

"Cops are on their way," Bennett seethes as he emerges from Lotti's and helps Tish off the ground, examining her reddened cheek. "I've got you." He easily turns her, moving a few feet away, glancing back at me then behind me. I feel who he's looking at before he says anything.

"What can I do?" Carter asks, leaning to catch my gaze.

"You can get this bitch off me!" the man in the choke hold rages as though Carter asked *him*.

"Two seconds and you'll be unconscious if you don't stop fighting me." I squeeze, but not enough where he can't respond.

"Okay. Okay," he rasps, relaxing in my hold, but I don't let up other than allowing him to freely breathe.

I should have been watching, paying more attention, not getting distracted by a handsome man wanting to talk to me, ask me out. Vigilant. Always have to be on alert, protect what's mine. "How you doing, Tish? You okay?"

"Yeah." She tips around Bennett so I can see her.

Carter reappears at their side, holding something out. "It's ice, for your cheek. Gently now," he encourages, guiding her hand to the side of her face, holding it until she has the ice-wrapped towel in place.

"Thank you." She sighs with relief. "I'm so embarrassed."

"None of that," comes from Bennett.

"You didn't do anything wrong," Carter offers at the same time.

Bennett's gaze meets mine. "How about you let me help you with him?" He motions to the asshole in my hold and steps toward me the same time as sirens near.

"I've got him." I meet Tish's gaze then Bennett's, and he nods, reading my intent.

He lowers his head, speaking softly. He's good with people. Better than I am. "Tish, it's up to you, but if you want a chance at stopping this treatment in its tracks, you need to press charges against Jimmy. The police are nearly here, and it'll be one of their first questions they ask you. I'd also recommend getting a restraining order. We can help with a lawyer if you don't have one."

"Really?" Tish is a lost lamb, shocked by any support or kindness.

"You're family," I remind her. "Family supports and protects each other."

"Thank you," Tish cries into Bennett's chest.

"We got you," he consoles her.

I catch Carter stepping way, pulling out his phone. I guess he has more important things to do than help out further. Though he did ask and I ignored him.

CHAPTER 5

NIGHTLY

HEART POUNDING, I HANG UP WITH COACH, thankful for the short reprieve. I still as I catch sight of the police officers closing in on Emmeline and the abusive boyfriend. Will they know who the bad guy is? Ready to intervene if they're thinking she's the perpetrator, I rush back to her.

One officer veers toward Bennett and the woman who was hit, and the other stops at Emmeline's side, meeting her gaze, assessing the situation. "Hey, Em. You doing our job for us again?"

"Officer Rourke." She nods in greeting. "I wouldn't dream of it, except Jimmy here decided to use Tish as a punching bag." She motions to the woman with Bennett. "He was causing a scene inside about thirty minutes ago. I interrupted, tried to deescalate. He left, but dumb can't help being dumb, and this asshat came back, deciding getting arrested was the way he wanted to start his morning."

"Alright." Pulling out his handcuffs, Rourke quickly secures the man's hands behind his back, stating, "Stay on your knees," before helping Emmeline to her feet. "You good?"

"Yeah, I'm good. I'm going to get Tish a water—"

"I need you to wait a second." He motions to her lip.

Shit, I didn't even notice she was bleeding.

The officer leans in, examining. "He do that?"

She tentatively touches her mouth, noting the blood on her fingers and frowns. "He clocked me with the back of his head as I was subduing him."

Gently, I touch her back, getting her attention. "I'll grab waters and some ice for your lip." I don't wait for a reply, but do hear the officer ask her if I'm a witness. I don't hear her response as the door closes behind me. I'll give my statement after I ensure Emmeline is okay.

Bennett greets me when I step outside with a bag full of bottled waters. I hand him one. "Are they doing okay?" I'm asking about Tish but especially wondering about Emmeline. She moved with the grace of a gazelle and the fierceness of a tiger with no concern for herself, got herself a busted lip for thanks in the process.

"Tish is going to have a shiner. They're taking her statement now. Let me take a couple of these waters." He nods to the towel in my fist. "Is that ice for Em?"

"Yeah, I'm just going to give her a water and the ice."

"Sounds good." He moves to Tish and the officer she's speaking to.

Approaching Emmeline and the other officer, I offer her the towel with ice, "For your lip," before cracking open a water and putting it in her other hand. "You need anything?" I ask as I offer a water to the officer.

"Thanks, man." He motions to Bennett. "He said you need to get going. Can you hang around to give your statement? Or you can come to the police station later."

Emmeline looks away, jaw clenched. She's either deep in it, fighting the adrenaline rush, or she's ticked at me. I'm not sure which, but I really do need to go. Coach's understanding only goes so far.

"If it makes no difference, I'll come by the station later." This season is a big one for us, and as the team captain, it's up to me to set the example. I told Coach I had to stay to make my statement, but if a few hours don't matter to the officer, then I'll take the out to make my commitment to the team.

"Sure, Mr. McNight, no problem." He hands me his card. I don't even stop to consider if he recognizes me or if Bennett or Em told him my name. "Call me when you're on your way."

"Thanks. I will." I pocket his card and turn toward Emmeline, gently touching her chin, gaining her eyes. She already stopped icing her lip. "You sure you don't need anything? I can stay a little longer if you want me to." I have my commitments, but already this woman feels like one of them.

Her brows arches. "Don't let me keep you from your important business." She all but dismisses me as she addresses the officer. "Let's get those pictures you need of my face and get my statement so I can get back to work."

"Em—"

"Goodbye, Mr. McNight." She slams the figurative door so hard, I feel it rattle in my bones.

EMMELINE

After we gave our statements, Tish insisted on going to work. She can't afford the time off even though we both offered to help her out. Her pride, and maybe a bit of fear, won't let her go home to an empty place to sit alone in the aftermath of this morning. Thankfully, she doesn't cohabitate with Jimmy. She lives a block over, in an apartment over Joe's Pizzeria. Bennett walked her to the vet's office, but not before talking to Nightly as he headed to his truck.

Inside Lotti's, I make the best of what's left of the morning, putting Mr. Tall, Dark, and Gorgeous out of my mind, or at least on the far back burner.

When next I look, it's lunchtime, and Bennett escorts me to our office to take a break and ice my lip after eating a bowl of soup that only makes it bleed anew. I can't believe I let that asshole get in a potshot like that. I didn't even remember it happening until Office Rourke pointed it out.

"What happened, Em? Why the cold shoulder?" Bennett questions.

"I'm not giving you the cold shoulder." I search through my desk drawers for tissue, when really, I'm just avoiding his knowing gaze.

He hands me the small ice pack we keep in the freezer. "Not me. *Him*. What did Mr. Dark and Dreamy do?"

"He *left*. He made a phone call as soon as the cops arrived. Dismissed us and went back to his busy hot-shot life… *and*, he distracted me."

"Really, Em?" He stretches out on the sofa that barely fits in here. He insisted we needed someplace to sit other than our desk chairs. He's not lying. It's good for a quick nap too, especially when working open to close, nearly seven days a week. It makes for long days and even longer weeks.

When I only shrug my response, he continues, "He was late for practice. He was already on the edge of late, waiting to talk to you in the first place—he thought you were worth it. He stuck around and helped without trying to take over. Why won't you give him a chance? I know you like him. What's not to like?"

"He's a celebrity."

"He's a pro athlete."

"Same difference."

"Maybe, but he's also just a guy asking you to go out with him."

"He told you?"

"No, you just did." He's so smug.

I wave him off. "I can't. That's not a life I want to be a part of." I search my phone and hold it up. "This is his life."

Bennett leans forward, grabbing my phone, scanning the article. "Em, it was a charity auction. All sports teams support a charity or two; many pro athletes even have their own charities. I can't believe you're holding this against him." He holds up the picture of Nightly with a tall, willowy blonde, and another guy, who looks to be the Denver Broncos' quarterback.

"He's famous."

"Hmm, he's famous-*lite*. He's *sports* famous, not worldwide famous like Brad Pitt, or nearly every other actor you've ever heard of. You didn't even recognize him when you first met him. He's not *that* famous—he can still go out in public and buy coffee. Don't hold his career against him."

Bennett's getting on my last nerve. "Why are you pushing this?" I just need to go home and indulge in a glass of wine and a long, hot bath.

"Because, despite yourself, you want a family. You want babies. He's a perfect specimen to give them to you. You two would make beautiful babies."

"You could give me your spunk. *We'd* make beautiful babies."

He cringes. "I love you like a sister, Em. I do not want to reproduce with you." He sits up and grabs my purse, holding it out. "Besides, I have my own dreams of a family, and it doesn't include you as my wife or baby-momma. I love you like my platonic soulmate, as the woman who got me through basic training and nearly every mission after that, saved my ass more times than I can count, and who I love dearly. But, no, my sperm is not going anywhere near your uterus." He shudders, literally shudders.

He's horrible for my confidence in my womanly wiles. I've nearly forgotten what it's like to be desired. B fills so many of my buckets, except that one.

I take my purse as I stand. "Are you sending me home?"

"I am." He types dramatically on his phone, then my phone pings with a text. "That's his number. You need to call him. Apologize for being a hard-as-nails Marine who doesn't know how to open her heart to a good thing."

"I'm not apologizing. He left."

"Em," he sighs. "He left to get to practice—his job, not to party. They get fined every minute they're late. He offered to stay for you, even though you were already freezing him out. Officer Rourke told him he could give his statement later, not like they really need it. They have yours, mine, Tish's, and nearly every customer near the windows. But given his reputation as a stand-up guy who's famous-*lite*, having his statement wouldn't hurt. Give the guy a break. Call him."

He kisses my forehead, grazing my lip with a finger. "And don't tell me again that he distracts you. That's the point. You could do with a little distraction. Find a life, Em, that's not this place. Go home. Have some wine. I'll bring by dinner later." He smacks my ass as I pass. "*If* you're a good girl and call him."

I nearly pout as I pull my sunglasses out of my purse and jangle my keys at him. "I thought you were on my side."

He laughs. "Darlin', if I wasn't on your side, I never would have followed you to Colorado, busting my ass every day, helping you make this business the success it is." He slides into my personal space, gripping my hand. "I love you, Puddin'. But you need to get out of your own way."

I leave, half-heartedly huffing my indignation all the way to my car. It's not like my bestie is dating anyone. I don't even know the last time he got laid. Not that I'm making a pie chart, but it's hard not to notice when we spend nearly every waking hour together and are neighbors. Both of us are kinda in the same boat.

If I *were* making a pie chart, it would only have one solid circle that said Lotti's Latte with maybe a sliver of taking a few hours a week to help out the neighborhood shelter and food bank. Though, I'm not sure the percentage is high enough to even register on the imaginary chart.

My lip throbs, and my righteousness has taken a beating. Maybe I am being a little too hard on Nightly, judging him for things I haven't witnessed firsthand.

Wine then bath.

Then maybe a phone call to a knight. Though, no promises on the apology front.

There, I have a little indignation to spare.

Is this a hill I want to die on, holding on like a crazed cat lady to her ideals with dried-up ovaries and a shriveled heart?

Not exactly the future I had planned.

CHAPTER 6

NIGHTLY

"YOU'RE LATE. THAT'S NOT LIKE YOU." TATE SKATES to my side as I make a lap, warming up, stretching out the knots and sleepy muscles with a groan. "Storm was hoping you wouldn't show."

I'm sure he was. I catch Storm's grinning mug from across the ice, doing his static stretches on all fours, which I need to be doing too. He's a skilled, good-hearted recent acquisition from the LA Legends, always hoping I don't show so he can be first-line center. As we near, I nudge him with the head of my stick. "Today's not the day, Storm."

Quick as lightning, he grabs the shaft, holding on till I swerve toward him to avoid a full-on tug-of war, and then lets it go. His smile only grows as I right myself, continuing my lap with Tate at my side.

"A guy can dream. It'll happen one day," Storm hollers over his shoulder.

True, it will, but hopefully not for a while. I'm not ready to shift down or hang up my skates. I have more to prove, and I really want to lead this team to the Stanley Cup.

"Nightly." Coach Alan waves me over then turns his focus to

Brady, our tech guy, motioning to his iPad. If there's something wrong with his tablet, he's going to be cranky. He's all about modern technology, until it glitches.

I nod to Tate, letting him know we'll catch up later. I ease up, slowing as I near Coach, not wanting to spray him with ice. "Hey, Coach. Sorry I'm late."

He holds up a finger, telling me to wait as he finishes up with Brady.

"Sure thing. I'll be back in a jiff." Brady tucks Coach's iPad under his arm, then looks at me. "Hey, Nightly."

"Hey, man." I barely spare him a glance, preparing for Coach to chew me out. He's a good man, patient until he's not. Nice until he's not, always with a reason.

When Coach turns, facing me full-on, his assessing gaze lingers on my face then down to my hands and back to my face. "You're okay? Any damage?"

"No, sir. I wasn't involved in the altercation, only a witness. I hung out long enough to help where I could and speak to the police. The officer agreed to let me come to the police station to give my statement after practice." I take a breath. Ramble much?

"That's good you were there to help. I'm relieved you weren't hurt. Will I see you on the news?" *Do I need to get the PR team involved?* is what I hear.

"I don't think so. It's just a local coffee house." I hate using the word *just* as it relates to Emmeline and her business. "Perhaps I should give Charlie a heads-up to be safe."

"Good man. I'll have Coop call the office to have her come down as soon as she can break free." He pats my shoulder. "Get back to warming up."

"Yes, Coach." I take the reprieve and get my head in the game. It's all about practice and not a frustrating miracle worker with coffee who twists me up and makes me doubt my own worth as a potential boyfriend.

Later, worn out but invigorated by a satisfying, cohesive practice, followed by lifting and cool down, I head for the locker room. Fresh from a shower, I barely get the towel around my waist before Assistant Coach Cooper calls me into Coach Alan's office. I grab another towel to dry my hair on the way.

I pause just inside his door, second-guessing my decision to not at least put on pants. Charlie Hudson, our head of PR; and our Social Media guru, Summer Black, meet my gaze across the room. We're all professionals here, yet I feel significantly naked in a room of fully dressed co-workers.

I ignore my discomfort. "Charlie, Summer, thanks for coming down."

Charlie leans against the small conference table in Coach's office, her gaze assessing. "Coach Alan tells me you have a situation I may need to be aware of?"

"I was a witness to a crime this morning…" I fill her in on the events at Lotti's Latte. Before I'm done, I see the gleam in Summer's eyes and head her off before she can push her Nightly-Do-Gooder Social Media Agenda. "It wasn't a robbery. It's domestic abuse, assault on a nice woman who frequents Lotti's. This is not an opportunity to exploit her pain and heartache in the guise of touting any misguided belief I'm heroic on our social media. I was not heroic. I'm not the one who stopped the assault in its tracks. I'm simply a bystander who witnessed the crime.

"I'm only letting you know as a courtesy in case anything pops up related to me. We should not be the ones to initiate a media frenzy by posting about a crime that doesn't involve me." Even if it did involve me, I would be loath to see it published on our social media. "I'm sorry, but the most heroic thing I did was bring everyone water and ice packs for injuries afterwards. There's not a sexy story here for you."

Summer's shoulders deflate. I know it's her job to look for stories in our everyday lives that humanize the players, the franchise. It shouldn't be at the expense of real people and co-opting their tragedy, though.

"I agree," Charlie chimes in, moving for the door with Summer in tow, thanking the coaches. She stops in front of me. "Thanks for the heads-up, Nightly. It's always better to be prepared for all contingencies. I'll write up a statement in the event something does come up. But don't sweat it. I doubt it'll be needed."

"Thanks." I shake her hand and then Summer's, mumbling, "Sorry." She's a great gal, maybe a little over eager to post new content that isn't about hockey.

"Don't be. You're right. But maybe you could save a cat in a tree or something later." She smirks. "And be sure to get video or at least a few pics."

I chuckle. Never going to happen. Not that I don't like cats. I like them fine. But the idea of doing it *and* making a video while I do it—and then posting that vid somewhere? Nah, not my style. "Sure thing."

With a nod and a dismissal from Coach, I get dressed, catching a few conversations about going out for drinks tonight. My stomach rumbles, reminding me I need to eat something before I go to the police station to give my statement. I tag Tate and Storm. "I want steak. You game to go to Dante's tonight?"

"Dang, didn't know you were a mind reader too," Storm teases.

"Too?" I gotta hear this.

Storm, grabs his duffel, slinging it over his shoulder. "Yeah, you know," he shrugs, "leaping over tall buildings in a single bound, rescuing women and children, helping out teammates when we lose our way—"

"Shut it." I rap him on the arm. "I'll meet y'all there, say seven? I've got an errand to run, but I gotta grab a snack or something first, or I'm going to be gerbil hungry by then."

"Eww," Storm fake gags.

"Man, you and food analogies—" Tate starts.

"Gerbil hungry?" Braydon joins us.

"Yeah, hungry enough to eat my young, like a gerbil." I lunge, pretending to take a bite out of his arm.

"Dude." Braydon shakes me off, laughing, his scowl relenting. "That's disgusting."

I grip his shoulder. "It truly is. You joining us for dinner?"

"Yeah. Thanks." He seems grateful for the invite. I don't know why, with Storm being his main friend, we usually invite him. He just doesn't always come.

We grab our gear, agreeing to meet at Dante's Steak and Chop House. I can't wait for that first succulent bite. Damn, I'm a hungry beast. I text Dante, letting him know we're coming to his place tonight. He'll have a table ready for us when we arrive. No waiting. A secluded corner table or booth where we can enjoy our dinner without fanfare.

There are perks to being a professional athlete. It doesn't hurt that we behave and tip well.

I make a food run, damming my hunger for a few hours before calling Officer Rourke to let him know I'm on my way to the station.

CHAPTER 7

EMMELINE

I GROAN AS I LOWER INTO THE SUDSY WARMTH OF my tub, relishing the jets as the water beats against my sore body. I haven't worked out in a while, been too busy—or not a priority—and my aching muscles are screaming at me to pay attention. *Do not neglect us*, they chime. *Yeah, yeah, I hear you.*

Tomorrow, I'm back to my workout routine, which means I either lose sleep, get to work later, or leave earlier. I know which will most likely happen and which will just get pushed until I decide I can go the next day or the next. That's why I'm in this situation. I kept putting it off, not making it a priority.

When did I become this lackadaisical, putting my health on the back burner? I've been a workout fiend since I was sixteen and realized my taller stature didn't mean I was equipped to defend against those who believe they have a right to touch what isn't theirs. Six months ago, I never would have missed a workout. A Marine never puts off what can be done today.

When did this happen? When did I stop even *thinking* about it? It's a miracle I'm not five sizes bigger than I am, given my penchant for sweets in the form of pastries and coffee drinks—hot or cold. My unit would laugh me off the track if they saw me huffing and puffing to make a mile. This is a disaster.

Locking up the memory of *why* I started running, working out, and learning self-defense when I was a kid, I dry my fingers and dial my bestie, putting him on speaker.

"Puddin', what's up?" Bennett's soothing voice settles the parts of me that rarely settle.

"When did I become a lazy blob?" I hear the touch of hysteria in my voice and breathe through the urge to restate my question at a saner volume.

He chuckles, then chokes on the dichotomy. "Come again? There's not a lazy bone in your body."

"When did we stop working out?" I've regained my composure.

"Stop?" he scoffs. "Darlin', I never stopped."

"What?! When? *I* can't find the time, and you're always with me. How do you manage it and I don't?" The incredulous volume is back.

A soothing *hmm* of understanding comes over the phone. "I'm not with you now."

"Are you working out now?" He can't be. I should stop this luxurious indulgence and join him. I sink in further, closing my eyes and breathing through the panic of being left behind, left out, forgotten. *He's not leaving me. He's working out, not moving to another country.* Working out for B is as important as breathing. I used to feel that way. It's always bonded us. I'm such a loser. Did I leave him behind, or did he leave me?

"Hey, hey, Em. What's going on?" His tenderness makes my heart hurt.

"Are you working out without me?" I'm pitiful. I'm supposed to be a strong independent woman, but in reality, I'm a well-trained retired Marine, who might be a little too co-dependent on my best friend, who can't even think of accepting a date with a nice guy when he asks.

"I just finished a jog. If you want, come with me tomorrow."

Or I could learn to do it on my own, not tie my workout routine to Bennett's. If I rely on myself, I only have my time, my schedule to contend with. But *his* schedule is basically *my* schedule. "I'll think about it."

"Okay." I hear water turn on in the background. He must be getting ready to shower. "What do you want for dinner?"

Dinner? I want a pity party with a side of cheesy hamburger, fries, and a mondo chocolate shake. None of which will Bennett provide. He doesn't believe in fast food. He cooks, like, all the time. I talked him into eating McDonalds once; we both regretted it, except the fries. I could never regret those fried gifts from the food gods.

"I think I'm just going to eat cereal and tuck in for the night."

"You sure? I don't mind—"

"Yeah, I'm sure. And do you think you could open in the morning? I'm going to work out before heading to Lotti's. If I wait till after work, I probably won't do it."

"Of course. Come in late, take the day off. Whatever you need, Puddin'."

Damn, he's such a great guy. Why couldn't we love each other in a non-platonic kinda way? He'll make a great partner and daddy someday. "Okay. I'll let you know."

"Em, are you okay?"

Don't ask that. I swipe at my leaky eyes. "Yeah, it's just the aftereffects of taking down a bad man."

"You did good today. You saved Tish." He doesn't bring up where I failed at being *good* to Nightly, and I appreciate it.

"Not good enough." I didn't save her from getting hit in the first place.

"Don't do that. You can't stop every abusive man from taking out his anger on others."

"I know." I do, but the guilt persists. I know what it's like to be helpless, to need a kind hand and not get it. I never want to feel that way again—or watch while someone else experiences it.

"But you'll still beat yourself up for not reading his mind and putting him down before he could even consider lifting his hand against her."

I shrug, making the cooling bath water tickle my ear. "Probably."

"Eat. Have that glass of wine. Put on a movie and call Nightly. He'll cheer you up."

That's a lot to put on him. But maybe... "Good night, Benny."

"Don't call me that." He sighs. "Night, Puddin'."

It's after seven when I put my bowl and spoon in the dishwasher. I ended up making Cream of Wheat, comfort food from my childhood when I was sick or Mom couldn't find anything I wanted to eat. Seemed like a better choice than cold cereal and wine. Drinking won't help me get up for a run in the morning. The lethargy, the headache will just be an excuse not to.

iPad in hand, I cozy up on the couch, determined to knock out a book from my TBR instead of watching brainless TV. Though my psyche could use a little brainless right now, escaping into a romantasy is even better.

Before I dive in, I grab my phone, pulling up the text from Bennett with Nightly's number and save him as a contact. Then, I decide to do something for myself, something I haven't done in a long time, except with Bennett. I ask for help. Nightly won't know it, of course.

His line rings several times before clicking over to voicemail. My heart sinks—do I leave him a message? Does he even know it's me calling? Did he save my number from my proposition note? If not, I could hang up, and he'd never know. But then I'll be left in the same boat of wanting to make a change and needing a little support to push me over the starting line from someone who's not my bestie.

Being brave, I hold my breath until his voicemail greeting comes over the line and take a solid breath when it beeps: "Nightly, it's Emmeline from Lotti's. Bennett gave me your number. I hope you don't mind. I…um, just wanted to…" Dang, why is this so hard? I can kill a man with my bare hands, yet asking him for a favor seems impossible.

I don't deserve the favor after the way I treated him today. Before I make even more of a fool of myself, I panic and hang up.

Shit. Shit. Shit.

Do I call him back to leave a more coherent voicemail? That'll seem desperate, right? What if he picks up? Then I'll have to explain why I called him twice without him having listened to the first message.

I jump when my phone rings and his name pops on the screen.

"Hello?" I answer before I chicken out and send him to voicemail.

"Hey, Emmeline. Nightly."

"Hi—"

"I'm sorry I didn't answer when you called. I didn't have your number in my phone."

Of course he didn't. He's not desperate enough to save a number from a card used to proposition him. I'm a dime a dozen.

"You there?" he asks after I've taken too long to reply.

He's somewhere busy based on the noises in the background. "Is this a bad time?"

"No, no. I'm out to eat with a few of the guys."

"Oh, yeah? Where?"

"Dante's Steakhouse. Have you been here?"

"No, but I love steak…" Shit. It sounds like I'm angling for an invitation.

"I'll bring you sometime, if you'd like."

Gah, I recoil. "I wasn't fishing for an invite."

I catch a soft laugh before he says, "I didn't think you were." He pauses, and I don't know how to fill the space. "So, your call, what can I do for you?"

I take a deep breath and leap. "Do you run? Can you meet me in the morning for a run? I mean, if you run and aren't busy. Shit. You're always busy with practice, huh. Never mind, it's okay—"

"Em, I'd love to meet you. What time? Where?" he cuts off my rambling, thank God.

"I don't know what's close for you. I can meet you wherever…"

His deep chuckle eases my nerves. "I live closer to Lotti's than the stadium, but I don't have practice until later, so I can meet you anywhere. Where do you live?"

I resist the urge to blurt out my address. I mean, desperate much? We settle on a park that's convenient for both of us. "Is seven okay? Too early?"

"No, it's perfect. Maybe we could grab breakfast afterwards. I know a place close to there."

Breakfast. Is it a date? A stinking, sweaty, after-running date? I've had worse. "I'd like that."

"Okay. I gotta get back to my friends, but I'll see you in the morning. Dress warm. It's supposed to be a cold one."

Dang. He's too sweet. "Sounds good. Enjoy your dinner."

"Thanks, you too. I mean, good night."

"Night, Nightly." I hang up, cringing at the night-Nightly word play. Too cutesy? He'll think I'm an unclever idiot.

A date. With Nightly. *Maybe* a date. But definitely restarting my exercise routine—or starting a new one. I laugh at the smile splitting my face and my silly heart thrumming in my chest like it has any idea what's at stake.

Is my heart at stake?

His blue eyes pierced into mine as he tipped my chin and iced my lip this morning. I've never… Bennett's the only man to show me such kindness. Or perhaps he's the only man I've *let* show me such kindness. Yet, Nightly just stepped right in, and I didn't balk. Though, I did dismiss him painfully quick.

Baby steps. Running then breakfast. Heart stuff later.

CHAPTER 8

NIGHTLY

I THOUGHT I WAS THE EARLY BIRD, SO SURE I'D BEAT Emmeline to the park with time for a good stretch before she showed. I couldn't be more wrong. By the sheen on her brow, she's had plenty of time for stretching and warming up. Maybe she's used to the early hours of the coffee house. The morning hours might not be as demanding as a bakery, but I imagine it's not too different.

Stealing a moment to take in the view, I'm hit by the grace and ease in her body as she moves from one stretch to the next. Comfortable in her skin, exuding confidence, yet a soft vulnerability from the bottom of her feet as she moves over the grass to the high arch of her hands as she reaches for the sky.

Beautiful. Gorgeous. Tall and lean. Agile and elegant. Breathtaking in her tight workout pants that hug her long legs and grip her hips and ass in a way that make me envious of them. Topped by a matching black jacket that doesn't look warm enough, but I imagine it is and even wicks away moisture, she's well put-together with a hip belt near her feet that holds two bottles of water. She came prepared.

She pops up from a stretch seconds before she spots me. "Oh, hey! Morning." Her smile's genuine if not a tad shy.

I step closer, sad my incognito ogling has come to an end, yet happy to move closer and catch the roughness of her morning voice. "Good morning." I go in for a hug as she puts out a clenched fist for a bump. We end up doing some sort of awkward side-hug fist-bump. We both laugh and step back, her gaze darting away, avoiding.

"It looks like you've warmed up. Give me a few minutes to stretch, and we can get going."

"Yeah, sure."

I focus on my movements instead of hers as she resumes her stretches. Otherwise, I'll be mesmerized all over again. I hold in my groans as I stretch. She doesn't need to hear my old-man sounds this early—or ever. Working out solely with guys has made me lax in decorum.

Once my limbs are loose and body warmed a few degrees, we set off down the path. I let her set the pace. I don't know her fitness level, and I don't want to push her to injury or have her doubt her ability to keep up. I've no misgivings she could put me down in ten seconds flat with the moves I saw her use the other day, but as for endurance, that is yet to be known.

"Do you run often?" She doesn't have earbuds in, so I'm hoping conversation is okay.

She catches me with a side glance before returning her attention to the path. "I used to. Honestly, I don't know when I stopped working out. One day seemed to turn into two, into a week." She shrugs. "I'm not even sure when the last time was. Months ago, sadly."

"You have good form. You're obviously in shape. I'm sure you'll return to your normal fitness level in no time." Bounce-back is a thing. Muscles have memory.

"God, I hope so."

"Are you okay if we keep talking, or do you prefer silence when you run?"

"Talking is fine, but I might get to a point where I can't." She motions to herself. "You know, out of the habit and all."

"Where did you learn to do what you did yesterday, those moves to take that guy down?" I wanted to ask her after it happened, but I think I was in shock and just trying to be helpful and not in the way.

"Mainly the Marines," she offers like it's no big deal, something she picked up in the skills section at the grocery store.

"Mainly?"

"I started caring about my fitness and ability to protect myself when I was younger. I got pretty good by the time I joined the Marines, but they honed my skills."

Honed is an understatement. It was impressive, not only how fast she moved but how quickly she disabled the guy, securing him on the ground. I've always thought I was in good shape, knew the way my body moves, but I'd look like a child playing at martial arts compared to her.

"Maybe you could teach me some moves sometime."

She full on turns, running backwards, studying me, brow furrowed. "Are you teasing me?"

"What?! No. I'm serious. It's impressive what you did, and I'm sure it's only a small inkling of what you can do. I know how to brawl, but not like that." I shake my head, driving home my denial. "I'd never tease about something like that. What you did for that woman—"

"Tish—"

"—was impressive."

She turns back to the trail, silently running beside me. I wonder if I offended her, but then she looks at me again. "Bennett would be a better teacher, but sure, I or we could teach you a few things."

"Did Bennett serve with you?"

"Yeah. We met in basic training." She picks up the pace, leaving me behind, her ponytail—and her ass—swishing from side to side. "Have you always played hockey?" She doesn't spare me a glance when I catch up a moment later.

"Mainly. I played some football and basketball in middle school, but hockey was my sport. My dad and uncles played and my younger brother too. My older sister played as a kid, but I don't remember seeing her play."

"You're like a hockey dynasty then?"

My laugh breaks free before I can stifle it. "Hardly… but…" Am I? "I've never really thought of it in those terms, to be honest. It was just something we did in my family, but it wasn't pushed on us. It was always around us and on the TV. My dad played Canadian hockey professionally for a few years before he followed my mom to Michigan, where she's a professor. He's a high school hockey coach, and my brother plays for the Chicago Chaos."

"I think that's a classic definition of a familial hockey dynasty," she teases, her breath more labored. I didn't really realize we picked up the pace again.

"You good? Do you need to slow down?"

She shakes her head but manages, "Maybe no more talking. I really want to make two miles today."

"Okay. You're in charge of the pace and how far we go. But we should take a right at the next split so we loop back to our cars instead of going farther if you're aiming for two miles. Otherwise, it'll be closer to five."

She only nods and digs in.

FACE-Off

EMMELINE

Breathing through the urge to puke, I slow and nearly stumble when I catch sight of my car. Thank God. My watch says we ran two miles, but if feels more like the five Nightly warned me of. How was I able to do that distance with hardly any effort? I'm embarrassed how out of shape I am.

"Here." Nightly tugs one of my waters out of the belt around my hips, popping the lid for me.

"Thanks," I manage before sucking down nearly half of it.

He gently touches my arm. "Keep walking so your muscles don't lock up."

I nod, trying to catch my breath. I know all of this, but damn, I just want to plop down and rest for a day or two. "I used to love running." I suck down air. "Now, I think it's a twisted, mean bitch."

Nightly's laugh brings a smile to my lips. "Yeah, sounds about right."

He encourages me to keep moving as I inhale deeply and let it out slowly, calming my heart. After a few minutes, we stop walking to stretch.

"Yeah, it's official. I hate running," I grumble.

"I swear you'll feel differently this time next week."

"You're assuming I'll subject myself to this again."

That gets me another laugh and a dazzling smile. I don't know how I didn't recognize him when he first walked into Lotti's. He looks just like he does on TV. As we ran, a few people did double-takes in recognition. He'd wave and keep going, not even a little fazed. It must be an everyday occurrence for him. Old news.

"You think you can make it to the black truck just there?" He points in the distance.

"Probably, but I'm over there." I motion to my SUV behind me, also black.

Sheepishly, he catches my gaze. "I was thinking I could drive us to breakfast and bring you back for your car afterwards."

"So, you were waiting till I'm worn out and slow to kidnap me?"

"Basically. What do you say?" The tilt of his head and the hope in his eyes is too cute to turn down.

"Lead the way, but if I puke in your car—that's on you."

He chuckles, catching my hand to help me off the ground where I hadn't gotten up from stretching. "Noted."

CHAPTER 9

EMMELINE

HE EATS HEATHY. IT'S INFURIATING. CAN'T I HAVE a man in my life who will indulge my love of junk food and all things sweet? He devours his egg-white omelet with more vegetables than I eat in a week. Add in dry wheat toast with avocado and straight *black* coffee, and it's my version of hell. His double side of bacon is the only clue he's human. Otherwise, I'm beginning to doubt his origins and what he did with the sweet treats he bought the first day at Lotti's. Did he try them or give them away?

There's not an ounce of fat on the man, which he boldly proved when we got to his truck. After helping me—the invalid—into the passenger seat, he yanked off his jacket and sweaty t-shirt, grabbed a towel from his bag in the back seat and began wiping off his glistening, ripped chest and abdomen without shame, rolled on fresh deodorant and donned a plain black t-shirt.

He didn't pay me a bit of notice, or mention the drool dripping from the corner of my mouth when he got in the driver's seat. Only a quick smile and a chipper, "Ready?"

I'm not sure I formed a coherent reply, but he seemed to understand my nod and drove us to this quaint diner near the park.

Close enough we could have walked. Thankfully, we didn't. My legs thank him.

Eyeing my apple caramel Dutch baby, he takes a sip of his offensive-to-my-soul coffee as I take another pleasure-inducing bite. Seriously, if I'd not had great sex in my life, I would think this is better (*than sex*).

The heated intensity in his gaze has me realizing perhaps I'm enjoying it a little too much. "Would you like a bite?" I prepare said bite, not waiting for a reply, and hold the fork out with my other hand below it to catch the dripping syrup.

Eyes locked on me, he silently leans forward and opens and closes his mouth around my fork. Lips tight, he slowly pulls back, revealing my empty fork one millimeter at a time. Jaw clenching and unclenching, he chews with the intensity of a million suns that heat my core.

Holy moly. I feel burned. I all but drop my fork and down what's left of my water, completely ignoring my sweetened mediocre dark roast. Then I lick off the syrup that dripped on my palm. His fingers twitch as if he's holding back from grabbing me and doing the same. God, that would be hot.

"Good?" I rasp, breaking eye contact to cut another mouthful for myself.

"Delicious." He balls up his napkin and pushes his empty plate aside. "Are you and Bennett together?"

"What?!" I cough around my mouthful, grabbing his water to wash it down since mine is empty. "Why would you ask that?"

His brow jumps. "You seem close. Are you seeing someone else?"

I frown at that. "I'm not the kind of woman who would hit on you if I was involved with *anyone*, much less my best friend."

"Just friends?"

"Yes," I bark, then soften my tone. "Bennett is my ride or die. If you have a problem with that, well—"

"I don't, as long as you two aren't—"

"We're not."

"Okay."

"Okay." I don't ask what I want to know: *Is* he *seeing someone?* Instead, I finish my food in silence, only relenting once I've had enough.

"Tell me about Lotti's. How did you go from the Marines to owning a coffee shoppe?"

Such an innocent question. Little does he know how stuffed with pain it is. "Lotti was my mom. She always dreamed of owning a place like that—well, almost like that. I've made some changes since I took over two years ago."

"Your mom…"

"Cancer. I was on active duty when she found out. As fate would have it, I was getting ready to re-up. Instead, I came home to take care of her and run Lotti's while she went through chemo."

"And Bennett?"

I narrow my eyes, trying to determine if he's really interested or still going down the path of investigating whether Bennett and I are more than friends.

He holds up his hands. "I'm trying to get to know you, Emmeline. You said yourself he's your ride or die, and he was in the Marines with you, so…"

Relenting, I release the tension in my shoulders and tell him the rest. "He came with. He's been a life saver—my rock. He would have re-enlisted if I did. We planned to do it together, but he came with me here instead."

"He's a good friend." No slight in that statement. Nightly means it.

"The best."

"And you two never thought of being more?"

Thought? Maybe. "We're not like that. He's my platonic soul-mate." Fiddling, I spin the salt shaker.

Nightly seems satisfied with that answer. "I'm glad you have him."

"Me too." I don't know what I'd do without Bennett.

"Any other family?"

"None that I know. My dad has never been in the picture. Other than a name, I know nothing about him." I shrug. "Never really cared, to be honest. If he doesn't want to be in my life, then I don't want to know him. Good riddance."

Nightly taps my hand, garnering my attention. "I'm sorry about your mom. I can only imagine how tough that was—is."

Yeah, I don't want to go down that path. He's seen me nearly puke. He doesn't need to see me cry. So, I simply nod my thanks, asking, "What about you? Mom and Dad are in Michigan, and your brother is in Chicago. Do you see them often? Where's your sister?"

"My sister is all over the place for her job. I see her more than anyone. My parents, not as much as I'd like. They're tied to the academic school year, so I usually see them over the summer. Sometimes they fly out for a game if it coincides with a school break. It's not like they're missing out since the games are on TV."

"Yeah, but you're their son. I'm sure they love to watch you in person to get to see you regardless of the hockey. Right?" I hope that's true. He's too nice of a guy to not have supportive parents.

"Maybe. They're busy, and my brother is closer."

"Do you see him often?"

"Not really, except when we play his team. He's not my biggest fan at the moment. He's trying to make his own mark on a team plagued with unruly teammates and bad press."

"I can image it would be hard growing up in your shadow."

He winces. "Yeah."

"Sorry. I didn't mean to touch a nerve."

"No. You're right. One of my teammates, Storm, he's in the same boat as my brother, working to get out from under the shadow of his twin who plays for the LA Legends. Witnessing his struggles has been eye-opening. I'd never really thought about it from their perspective. It's enlightening." He cares. Just the thought softens my heart a little.

"Have you shared that with your brother? I'm sure he'd appreciate it. Everyone likes to feel understood—seen. Even if you can't change his circumstances, just knowing you're here if he needs you could make a world of difference."

His smile is slow and tender. "You're a wise woman."

I shake my head. "No. I've got a great best friend who loves me on my worst days and praises me on my best. I want that for everyone in some form or fashion. You deserve it. So does your brother."

"I'm liking Bennett more and more."

My laugh is entirely too loud. "Don't tell him. His ego is big enough."

Back at my car, Nightly leans in, cupping the side of my face as he presses a kiss to the opposite cheek. Soft, warm lips invade my senses, awakening the need to feel his mouth on mine, tender and uninhibited. He surprises and calms me all at once.

Lingering, he breathes in deeply, causing a shudder along my spine and my hands to fist his t-shirt at his waist. "You smell amazing," he rasps.

His words tickle my ear, and the edge in his voice steals my breath, yet I argue, "I smell like sweat." There can't be anything attractive about that. Yet, he was sweaty too, and he smells amazing, like virile man and warm hugs.

He tips my chin, brushing his thumb along my bottom lip, still healing from the head butt from Jimmy. "You smell like endurance and bravery to me."

Holy mother of all that made this world. He's charming my panties off. If I was prone to trusting men, of wrapping them up and storing them in my most favorite place on earth, I'd keep this one.

"Tomorrow? Same time?" He steps back, physically releasing me from his hold, yet I still feel enraptured in all that is Carter Nightly McNight.

"Sure," I'll agree to almost anything if he keeps staring at me like he wants to wrap me up and keep me too. *Same, bud. Same.* Once I get a full breath, turning to unlock my door, I concede, "That is, if I can walk."

His laugh follows me as I get in my car with his parting words, "Call me if you can't, and I'll carry you."

He's teasing. Right?

"See you tomorrow, Em."

"Tomorrow," I promise before I second-guess the logic or the need to reinforce the wall around my heart from the likes of him—famous, with the world ready to bow at his feet.

I don't bow, and I don't do public.

CHAPTER 10

NIGHTLY

I'M KICKING MYSELF FOR NOT ASKING HER OUT TO something more romantic or official. Running together isn't exactly a date. But she agreed to go again.

I'm not sure what prompted last night's call to go running today. I'm glad she did. She's braver than I was. I'd planned to show up at Lotti's again after a few days, give her time to cool off from whatever I did to turn her off yesterday. It's possible it wasn't about me at all. The abusive situation between that couple would have rattled anyone, even a Marine. It could have been so much worse if Emmeline hadn't been there to stop it.

I should've told her how remarkable she was, so fast, selfless, and brave. Her quick action makes even more sense now that I know of her military background. The abusive boyfriend was smaller than me but quite a bit larger than Em, and she took him down like it was nothing. Even with her experience and skills, the attack could have rattled her in ways I don't understand, brought up memories or just reinforced how tenuous relationships and life can be.

It wouldn't be like that with us. I can prove it—if I can get her to give me a chance.

"Nightly!" Coach's whistle and bark rip my attention back to practice.

"Yes, Coach?" I whip around to face him.

He points to the other end of the ice where the scrimmage is happening while I was skating in circles around my goal like it's a Sunday stroll.

"Shit," I mumble.

"I tried to get your attention." Davi, our goalie, smiles, shooing me along.

"On it." I get in gear and take off for the puck, to the other goal to score on Tate. Poor guy. I've got a point to prove, and he just might be collateral damage. I'll make it up to him, somehow.

I steal the puck from Storm—*sorry, man. You're also on the wrong scrimmage team today*, pass it through Kells's skates, catching it on the other side, and pass to Alec, who whips around Evan, easily scoring on Tate.

"Nice assist. Thanks for finally joining us today, Nightly," Coach imparts from the bench. "Good job, Alec." Then he turns his focus on the losing scrimmage team. "Storm, Tate, Kells, wake up. Nightly wasn't even playing for half of that, and you still didn't manage to get the puck to the other end." He points at my goal. "Davi is bored as fuck."

I hide my smile as I imagine Davi's voice in my head, *Nah, Coach. I'm good.*

Alec taps my stick with his. "You good, man?"

"Yeah, all good. I'm here." My focus is where it needs to be.

"Thanks for giving me the shot," Alec continues as we reset.

"We're a team. It's my job to set you up to succeed." I could have taken the shot, but the objective is to practice working together, not furthering my individual agenda set by my ego. His goal *is* my goal.

Coach barks the next drill he wants us to focus on. I take the face-off and maneuver to deliver for my team.

I groan as I stretch out on the couch, Sports Center on in the background, laptop resting on my thighs. I tap out a few replies to emails, namely those from my agent, Austin, and my personal PR person, Angela, circling back around on the whole Lotti's abusive boyfriend incident. I'd called Austin on my way to practice yesterday to give him a heads-up. He in turn called Angela to fill her in so I wasn't later than I already was to practice. So far, there's been no media on the incident. I don't expect there to be, but it's good to be prepared.

A quick text from Austin reminds me of the charity event at the end of next month, offering to *hook me up* if I want a date. I love the guy, but I don't need his meddling in my personal life, though it's more public persona he's wanting to feed. I haven't taken a date to a charity event in years, not since I stopped sleeping around. But now, I'm wondering…

I hover over Emmeline's number, curious if she'd go with me. It's not a big deal. It wouldn't mean we're dating. Though the media might make more out of it if I show up with a woman on my arm after all this time, making it seem as though we were a couple. How would she feel about that? How would I?

Maybe by the time the event rolls around, we'll be an item.

Pride fills my chest. I'd like that a whole lot, too much for having just met her.

Instead, I send a text. Not about the charity event.

ME: *How are you feeling? Sore?*

Not waiting for her reply, I send the next message before I change my mind.

> **ME:** *Would you like to come to Saturday's home game, as my guest? Bennett can come too if you don't want to come alone.*

I set my phone aside and stare at the TV, trying not to think about her reaction or what mine will be if she says *no*. Distracting myself, I reply to Austin's text, letting him know I'll be going stag to the charity event.

Before I can set my phone back down, it pings. My heart races at the sight of her name on the screen.

> **EMMELINE:** *I am sore, but doing okay. I had a little more energy today. I forgot how that felt.*

> **ME:** *That's good. You're on the right track then.*

Do I sound condescending, like I know best? She's a friggin Marine. She doesn't need me telling her how important exercise is.

> **EMMELINE:** *That's debatable, but I'll do it again for another taste of that Dutch baby.* 😊

> **ME:** *It was pretty darn good.*

In all honesty, I wanted another bite as soon as the sugary goodness hit my tongue. I was trying to be good, impress her with my clean eating. In the end, I was just envious of her breakfast choice, though I would have been dragging at practice had I indulged.

> **EMMELINE:** *As for the game, we're in. Thanks for the invite. What time should we be there?*

I quickly shoot off the details for Saturday's game.

ME: *I'll transfer the tickets now. You'll get a notification on your phone. You'll need to accept them and then save to your phone to scan the QR code at entry. I'll include a parking pass in the reserved section. Let me know if you have any problems.*

She's a smart woman. I doubt she'll have trouble. I quickly access our team app, select two tickets and a parking pass, add her name and cell. Done.

EMMELINE: *Sounds good. Thank you again.*

We text for a few more minutes about her day and the possibility of having to buy a new espresso machine as it broke down again today. Then she needed to go eat. I check the timer for the oven, knowing my dinner will be ready soon too. We actually have a game tomorrow night, but I'd rather her come to a Saturday game, where I'm hoping to hang out with her afterwards and not have to worry about practice on Sunday since we're off.

I eat in silence, TV on in the background but muted for a call with my parents. They're going to Slade's game this weekend in Chicago. I'm not jealous. He's closer and needs their support more than I do, but them choosing to come here wasn't even a consideration.

I hadn't really thought about it until Em pointed it out, but now I'm noticing the difference in how they show up for us. They've only made a few of my games and mainly my first few seasons playing for the Colorado Dragons. It's disappointing more than anything else. My sister has been to more of my pro games than them.

Thinking of Willa, I send her a quick text. I'm pretty sure she's in the air right now, based on the schedule she sent me of her month. When she can, she builds in a stopover in Denver.

The evening feels heavy. The high of texting with Emmeline having passed, my empty house seems too cavernous and lonesome. A few weeks ago, I believed I was content in my life, happy I was no longer banging whoever offered. I never had to work at a hook-up, but then, neither did they. It was pretty easy. Too easy. I've felt the pang of wanting more out of my life, ready to find the one and settle down, have a few kids, a house, roots, traditions.

Now that I've met Emmeline, it feels closer yet even further away as I don't know if she's open to any of that, and it's way too soon to even consider those discussions. I need to get her out on a real date or at least over here where I can cook her a meal and really get to know each other.

She told me to call her sometime for a *ride*. What if I want forever?

CHAPTER 11

EMMELINE

WE DIDN'T MAKE THE FIRST GAME HE INVITED me to. I chickened out, said something came up last minute, but I showed up at the park for our run at the same time the next day, and the next, and the next. I've felt like shit—chicken shit—ever since, but he didn't hold it against me, just continued to invite me, continued to make our daily runs when his practice times allowed or he wasn't out of town for games.

I'm done being a scaredy cat. It's been three weeks of running, talking, sharing heated glances and teasing touches over breakfasts. I chose a few less sugary meals even though deep down I wanted that lovely Dutch baby again and again. I want him too.

Tomorrow is the night. B and I are going to Saturday's home game. No chickening out this time!

I've never been a huge hockey fan, but having Nightly in Lotti's and at the park, I feel a connection to the team I didn't have before. I don't know what we're doing. I'm trying not to think about it too hard. He's a nice guy. He's attentive, but other than the lingering kisses on the cheek in greeting and goodbye, there's been no other move to take it to the next level. Every time we part, I feel his absence, wishing for a true kiss, at least.

He's also never asked me out for another date. Maybe that's what our runs and breakfasts have been. If so, we've been dating for nearly a month. If not, I'm not sure going to his hockey game counts as a date. He's working. Playing hockey is technically his job. When he pops into Lotti's to see me—get coffee—I don't consider that a date. I very much doubt he does either.

I propositioned him first; maybe I also need to make the next move, especially if he felt rejected or like I was giving him "a sign" by not showing up to the first game. If I leave it up to him, I might be an old lady before I know if he even likes me like *that*. Tomorrow night, Bennett will have to go home by himself. I'm going home with Nightly and seeing what happens. It's settled.

Save a horse. Ride a hockey player.

I text Bennett as soon as I park behind Lotti's:

ME: *Here.*

BFF: *On my way!*

We get the clothes, pastries, sandwiches, and bushels of apples and bananas loaded in the back of my SUV and head out.

"How was your run?" Bennett's eyes never leave his phone.

"It was good. Better. My endurance is improving." I've bounced back faster than anticipated. I need to start doing weights and combat training again, stretch *those* muscles now that my stamina has improved. I'm still a long way off from where I was. It's a testament to how comfortable I am in my life. I feel safe, which is a good thing. Yet, letting my guard down when it comes to self-defense is not.

"How long are we staying today?" He hasn't looked at me once.

"Do you not want to go? I can go by myself. You don't always have to come with." I am capable of doing things by myself. Have I given him the impression I'm not?

"I made a commitment too." The censure in his tone has me second-guessing our *commitment* to the shelter.

Did he actually? Is his commitment to the shelter or to me?

"Hey," I pull over, haphazardly parking. I face him and wait.

He grabs the handle to get out, and it takes a second, but he finally looks up from his screen, noting we've *not* arrived at our destination. His furrowed brow lands on me.

"Em, why'd you stop?" He glances out the back window. "Are you even out of the road completely?"

I only shrug, eyes locked on him. Waiting.

"Em! Move. You're gonna get us killed parking like this. Some asshole could come by and hit your side of the car." The concern in his tone is a relief, but it doesn't explain what's going on with him.

"I'll move once you tell me what's up. You won't even look at me."

His eyes lock on mine, tenderness and urgency greeting me. "I'm looking at you now. Please, Puddin', move your car."

"Then you'll talk?"

He pockets his phone and nods. "Then I'll talk."

I drive us the rest of the way to the shelter, parking but not getting out.

"Can we go in, do this, talk after?" He undoes his seatbelt, touching my hand on the console between us. "I promise."

"Why not now?"

"I'd rather have a drink and privacy and more than twelve seconds we'll have while we walk from the car to the shelter. It's not bad. I just… I miss my best friend who ditched me for a guy."

"I have not!" I would never.

"You have. You've seen him nearly every morning, come in late—"

"You told me to come in late."

"One day. Not for the rest of eternity!" He lets out a tight breath. "Please can we do this later? We don't have time to talk about my stupid feelings."

Damn. Have I disappeared on him—on Lotti's? If I had other friends, would they say I've bailed on them too? "Your feelings aren't stupid. They're important to me." I squeeze his hand and turn the car off. He's right. This is not the time nor the place. "We'll talk later."

We meet at the back of my car, and I wrap him in a hug, mumbling, "Love you," into his chest.

He embraces me back, holding tight. "Love you too, Em."

"Hey, Joey. How are you doing?" Bennett and I just finished unloading the fresh food made specifically for the shelter and clothing we collected from the giving box placed in the dining area of Lotti's.

Joey, the man who makes everything and everyone work at Raven's Hope, smiles, checking out all the goodies. "I'm good, Emmeline. How are you guys?"

"We're good," Bennett chimes in. He catches my eye and smiles. We're okay—or we will be as soon as I quash whatever worries he has about me and anyone other than him.

I guess our co-dependance is shining through. We've been through a lot together, both on the battlefield and off. We're each other's emotional support animal.

"You've been busy." Joey waves over a few regular staffers to start organizing and putting everything where it needs to be.

I hand Joey an envelope. "A little something extra." I know he needs it.

"Em." He eyes the sealed envelope, making no move to open it. Then folds it and puts it in his back pocket. "I don't know what we'd do without the two of you."

I don't know either. This place is hanging on by a thread, going month-to-month, sometimes week-to-week. We do what we can, but still, it's not enough. "You get in a jam, call us. We'll do what's necessary to keep your doors open." It's not the first time I've offered, but it deems repeating as many times as Joey needs to hear it to trust he's not in this fight alone.

He swipes at his eyes. This place is more than job for him—for *everyone* that walks through these doors. He's a saint who's dedicated his life to serving others. First in the Army, now on the streets. It's a tough, thankless job, and he's a miracle worker with those in need of a one.

"I have a guy—Tom Waters. He's a good man, been stateside for about a year, young kid. Having a hard time transitioning back to civilian life. He's worked in kitchens his whole life, primarily a line cook, but he's willing to do anything, dishwasher, cleaning. He just needs patience and a steady job to get back on his feet."

Bennett pats Joey's back. "Is he here? Can we meet him?"

"No, he went for a job interview a few hours ago. I'm a little worried it didn't go well. He's not back yet."

"Give him my number, or he can stop by Lotti's anytime. We'll put him to work, see what he needs and make it happen." Bennett comes to my side, wrapping his arm around my waist. "Now, what can we do to help you out? We've got a few hours."

"We're all yours," I add, taking a deep breath, feeling the rightness of the situation. Bennett and I made it out of the military relatively unscathed. We're not perfect, but we have each other to get us through the hard times. Many don't have anyone. We do what we can to give back, and supporting Joey, his shelter, and the people he sends our way is the least we can do.

"I need twenty more people just like you two," Joey teases.

An idea forms. Maybe I know a certain someone who knows many someones who would be willing to lend a hand either physically or financially.

We get to work helping Joey and his team as I ruminate on my idea.

Later, as Bennett makes dinner, I pay bills and work on payroll. Most of it's automated, but I still like to review, stay on top of our budget, ensure the recorded hours match the schedule, and confirm there are no errors in the automated system before approving. Once I'm done, I slip onto the barstool at his kitchen bar and take a moment to appreciate the savory onions, meat, and many more smells I can't distinguish. They make my mouth water and my stomach rumble in anticipation. He's a maestro in the kitchen, and I look forward to every bite.

I dig into the roasted chicken and vegetables, savoring a sip of the paired wine Bennett selected. I'm reminded how well-suited we are for each other, how comfortable, how safe. "Why couldn't we have fallen in love?"

It's not the first time we've had this discussion. We're so close. We love each other, but we're not attracted to one another in that way. Our connection is soul-deep, but not sexual. Never has been, not even when I noticed his handsome face from across the room day one of basic training. We were drawn to each other from first glance, like a long-lost twin—twin souls, maybe.

"I do love you." He wipes his mouth and kisses the side of my head.

"I love you too, but I don't want to have sex with you." I fork a potato and shove it in my mouth before I contemplate the sex thing further. I can talk to him about it, but not envision doing it with *him*.

He calmly refills his glass then adds a bit more to mine. "Why are we rehashing this? We know what we are to each other and what we're not."

"Because I hurt you, and I don't ever want that to be the case. It would be so much easier if we were each other's person." I sigh and push my plate away.

"You *are* my person." He smiles and shrugs. "But I know what you mean. It would be easier we were in love love."

"I don't know how to spend time with someone new who I *do* want to have sex with, and not leave you feeling neglected." This is why casual sex has been my MO for so long. Though, it's been a while since I've even done that. I guess I stopped exercising and hooking up around the same time. I don't even remember why, other than feeling like I have no time. My focus is Lotti's and doing everything I can to help Joey and Raven's Hope.

"I'm sorry. I don't mean to be a burden. Maybe you could let me join you both occasionally, or run with me on days he can't." His tone is pained and telling.

I grip his chin, turning his beautiful face. "I need you to hear me." I wait until he's focused on me and nods. "You never have been nor ever will be a burden. It is my honor and privilege to be your friend. You're my other half, my twin-heart."

He removes my hand and grips it fiercely. "*My* twin-heart."

"I'll do better. I won't see Nightly after tomorrow." I don't know how I'll manage to do that and also ask him for help with Raven's Hope, but I have to try. Joey and his wards are desperate, and I only have so much time, money, and energy to offer.

"No. Don't you dare stop seeing him." Bennett picks up our plates, rounding the counter. "I'll work on being okay with not having you all to myself."

"Is that really it, though? Not wanting to share me?"

The groove between his brows only deepens as he considers my question. "No. I still want to spend time with you even if he's around. It's not a him *or* me. It's more of a *we*." He shrugs, not understanding our connection any more than I do.

We've been this way for so long, survived and recovered from our own traumas together, that healing has tied us to each other forever. It would be like amputating an arm or a leg to pull away from him now. Though, I admit Nightly fills a part of me that's allowed me to spend more time away from Bennett than I have in the past—and feel like the world isn't ending but expanding for once. Maybe the answer is finding Bennett someone too.

"We'll figure it out," I promise.

CHAPTER 12

NIGHTLY

I'M ITCHING TO GET BACK ON THE ICE. WE finished warming up and returned to the locker room until the start of the game ten minutes ago, and Emmeline and Bennett weren't in their seats. It doesn't mean they're not here, or not coming, and still, I'm anxious to know if she is. She canceled on me last time. No reason. She just couldn't make it.

I didn't push. It took weeks of meeting up to run and have breakfast for her to agree to come tonight. I hate that I'm nervous she won't come and even more nervous she will.

"You good?" Tate nudges me, motioning to Coach getting ready for his peptalk.

"Yeah, just wondering if Em is coming." I've never had a woman in my seats who wasn't my mom or sister. Not that anyone in the seats around them would know for sure they were with me unless they ask or Emmeline or Bennett mention it. Name-dropping doesn't seem like their style. Attendees in that section are usually WAGs, wives or girlfriends of the players, which is good, it keeps them protected, and security knows that section is for friends and family—they watch out for them in case it's a particularly rowdy game. Fans can be nuts sometimes.

"The chick from the place with the coffee you keep bringing in, right?"

"Yeah, *Emmeline* and her best friend *Bennett* are coming." At least I hope they are.

I've said those words before, and then she canceled. She didn't just no-show, but I'd already told some of the guys she was coming. I had to eat dirt when she didn't. I was more embarrassed than hurt. Doubted my ability, my worth to be more to her. But then I remembered we all have insecurities that show up in different ways. Trauma too, and she's been to war. Maybe hers is doing new things or crowds bother her. Or maybe something came up with Lotti's, and she truly just couldn't swing the time away, especially both of them.

"They weren't out there when we were warming up?"

"I didn't see them." Doesn't mean they aren't here somewhere, though.

He motions Paul over. As our equipment manager, he'll be with us the entire game on the bench.

"What's up?" Paul asks Tate.

"Our captain here has guests coming, and he just wants to know if they've arrived. Can you send someone out there to check?" Tate looks at me, and I rattle off their seat numbers.

"Can you also give them passes to come to the family area afterwards and someone to direct them?" I add.

"Course, Nightly. It'll be taken care of. Consider it handled." He darts off, speaking to one of our runners, who then rushes out the door.

"Can you focus now?" Tate draws me back to him.

"Yeah. I'm here. I'm focused." I stretch my neck and let out a puff of air. "I'm here," I repeat, working to put her out of my mind.

If I want to be more for her, I have to stay true to my team. I've got commitments and a reputation to uphold. I'm their captain. If I can't keep it together while having a relationship off the ice, I'll be a shit-poor example for my teammates.

I'm focused. I'm here. I hope she is too. The adrenaline is riding me hard. I'm so ready for this game, to feel the ice beneath my skates and wielding the puck like it was meant for me. We got this.

EMMELINE

"This is insane," I whisper-yell to Bennett. I've seen The Colorado Dragons' stadium on TV, but nothing prepared me for stepping down into The Lair. The outside is slightly domed, like the back of a black dragon, with glowing red lights between its scales and smoke escaping into the air. Inside, the arena is actually below ground. It has a cave-like feel even though it's a wide-open cavern. The tunnels leading to the ice are arched and painted like rock, or maybe they actually are rocks smoothed out to remove any rough surfaces. The lighting is insane, and the music is pulsing through my body. I want to dance—and I *don't* dance. I can, but I don't.

"It's intense," Bennett agrees, greeting a few people sitting around us. From their brief discussion, it seems we're sitting in the friends and family section. I'm honored. "Aren't you glad I bought you that jersey?" He motions to my shirt.

"Um, sure." I laugh. "If that makes you feel better." I fought him on it, but in the end, it felt like I was fighting him because I was worried what Nightly would think of me showing up with his jersey on. Would he be flattered, or fear I'm a stalker, or worse, a puck bunny just looking to score a new player? It helps that Bennett is wearing the same jersey, and as I take in the fans, we're not the only ones in Nightly or other team members' jerseys.

"Ms. Weston?"

Bennett leans forward, blocking me from the guy approaching from the aisle. "Can we help you?" He sounds anything but helpful. I grip his arm, letting him know I'm okay. *He's* okay.

The young man isn't fazed. I'm sure he's used to protective assholes working here—according to his nametag—among the hockey players. "I'm Brooks with Player Relations. Mr. McNight asked me to check to see if you needed anything and to give you these." He holds out passes. "They're for the family room after the game. I'll come back to take you there near the end of the third period."

I reach past Bennett for the passes. "Thanks." I was wondering how we'd meet up with Nightly with all the fans. There has to be close twenty thousand people here. I could have asked Nightly, but a part of me wondered if we should just leave at the end since he didn't specifically ask to see me—us—after the game. Again, not knowing if this is a date or not, I didn't want to push and feel stupid.

"If you need anything, just tell Tony or any of the security guards for this section, and he'll get in touch with me."

"Thank you." He's really making me feel important here. I'm nobody special, though I guess it's obvious our connection to Nightly grants us this treatment.

"It's my pleasure." Brooks greets a few other people in our section before disappearing into the nearest tunnel.

"That was interesting." Bennett leans into me, giving me comfort I didn't know I needed. There are a lot of people here. If it wasn't so expansive, I'd be claustrophobic. Thankfully, the seat next to me is empty, for now.

Bennett buys us waters and popcorn from a passing vendor only moments before the house lights dim and the intricate laser light show begins with thrumming music as the announcer comes on over the speakers welcoming us to The Lair.

NIGHTLY

I don't spot Em until I'm introduced and skate onto the ice. I circle around, scanning through the lights and fog to find her on her feet with Bennett at her side, clapping and cheering us on.

My heart races for a whole other reason. I've never had anyone not related to me cheering for me, at least who I knew and cared about beyond appreciating the fans. Pride fills my chest, and I want everyone to know she's here for me.

My eyes lock on her jersey, finding my number plastered across her chest. My smile only grows as I take in Bennett's matching jersey. They come as a pair—and he's being supportive. I'm not sure what to do with that realization as I join my team for the national anthem.

Focus. Now's not the time to hash out the baggage that comes with wanting to date Emmeline.

Giving her one more glance, I point my stick in her direction, as if to tell her *I see you; I'm glad you're here; this win is for you.* I hadn't planned on doing that, making it so public that I have someone in the stands. The crowd on her side turns, in one choreographed move, trying to locate who I'm pointing to.

Will she hate me for this, especially if they figure out it's her? I swear she blushes. Never thought she'd be the type. That empty hole in my chest fills a little more. I want this to be a regular thing. I want to be a familied-up player who has someone incredible rooting for them, and warm, comforting arms to fight for, come home to.

With determination burning through me like the sun, I face off with the LA Legends' center. He's new to their team, but I've met his challenge before. Seconds before the ref drops the puck, I lean in. "Sorry for making you look bad, Stu."

"What—"

I've got the puck, slipping around behind Evan on our defense and passing it up to Kells, left wing, and we break away toward their net. The crowd goes wild, and somewhere in the deep recesses of my mind, I allow myself to think I hear Em's voice cheering me on.

EMMELINE

I'm hoarse from screaming and cheering. My heart races, and I clutch Bennett's arm as Nightly makes another goal with assists from Alec and Kells—according to the announcer. All I saw was the puck flying between them, and then Nightly tipped it past the goalie into the net like it was nothing. Just a simple tap and the crowd goes insane, music blares, and Nightly lifts his stick to me, as he has with every goal he's made. Connecting us.

I'm enthralled, in deep, and want to screw his brains out.

"Dang, girl. Keep it in your pants," Bennett teases as though I said it out loud.

I slap his arm, telling him to hush.

He only kisses my cheek. "I'm happy for you."

And I know he is.

I'm happy for you rings in my head as the game ends—the Dragons win—and we're led through the masses to the family room where we wait for Nightly.

CHAPTER 13

EMMELINE

"DO YOU FEEL LIKE WE'RE ON DISPLAY?" BENNETT leans in as we hold up the wall farthest from the door we entered through.

"A bit." I turn my shoulder to the wall, facing my bestie. "Thank you for coming with me. I'm not sure I could have done this without you."

"You could have, but I'm happy I came. It was fun." His gaze returns to the room. "They can't all be wives. I mean, some dress like they could be, but others look like they just stepped off the stripper pole." He shrugs when I glare at him. "Sorry, but it's true."

It is. Same with the fans. Some were normally dressed. Others went all out with face and body paint, no shirts for some guys and barely-there tops—or bottoms, for that matter—for the girls. I'm thankful we only went so far as to wear jerseys. I'm not up to tramping it up for Nightly, at least not in public. I'm a friggin' Marine. I worked hard to be taken seriously as a woman in a male-dominated world. Dressing with my tits and ass hanging out is nowhere on my list of to-dos. *If* I were inclined to do so, it would be for my comfort and no one else's gaze.

"They're coming." Bennett stands to his full height, pressing into my side when I do the same. "I'm leaving as soon as we say hi."

My gaze flicks to him. "What?! No."

He tips my chin. "Puddin, you need this."

"But I…" Confidence leaves me on a rush of air, my heartbeat pounds in my ears, and my eyes water. I clench my fists. I will not cry.

"You what? Want me to hold your hand during?"

I bark out a laugh. What is wrong with me? "That'd be too much, even for us."

"He's here." Bennett nudges my shoulder.

I look over just in time to catch Nightly's gaze from across the room as he's congratulated by others, claps on his shoulders and back, yet his eyes never leave me as he makes his way to us. The intensity of his stare mixed with pure want lay ruin to any doubt I still hold that he's not attracted to me.

He stops in front of us. "Hey, beautiful." Leaning in, he kisses my cheek. "You always smell so good," he whispers before pulling away, his touch lingering. "Hey, Bennett." Nightly holds out his hand. "Thanks for coming."

Bennett eyes Nightly's hand for a second before accepting it. B's not big on contact with strangers. Maybe he doesn't consider Nightly a stranger anymore or just doesn't want to be rude to the guy whose jersey we're wearing. "Thanks for inviting me. Great game."

"It was an amazing game." I force a smile, maybe a bit too eager to prove I'm not freaking out. Bennett is leaving, my comfort zone. I'll be left with Nightly, who represents so much of what I want, yet haven't had the guts to pursue before. Can I do this? Maybe B *could* hold my hand during…

Nightly notices. I'm coming to realize there's not much he doesn't notice. "You okay?"

"Yep. All good." My pitch is still too enthusiastic.

"Listen, I'm gonna head out." Bennett thumbs over his shoulder, like that's the direction he's supposed to go when the door is the other way. "You two have fun. Thanks again for including me."

Already? "Wait—"

"You want to join us?" Nightly asks Bennett before checking in with me. "I thought we could grab a bite, or if you'd rather, I could cook something at my place."

"Oh, nah, man. Third wheel and all," Bennett brushes off the invite so smoothly, like he doesn't want to stick around, yet I read in the tenseness of his jaw and the crease in his brow, he wants to stick with me.

Before I can protest further, Bennett wraps me in a hug. "Be brave, Em," he whispers, then pulls back. "I'll see you tomorrow." He shakes Nightly's hand again and rushes out the door.

There's ringing in my ears. Are the walls closing in?

Nightly's attention falls to me. "Emmeline—" His blue gaze calms my panic.

"I guess… he…" I fall silent, lost to find words to describe what Bennett's feeling. What *I'm* feeling. It's too much to encapsulate though. Too friggin much. I want to jump from watching B leave to being alone with Nightly. I don't want this discomfort of finding my footing without my best friend cheering me on, holding me up when I'm not steady, and reminding me I'm not broken in so many ways I know I am.

Breathe, Em, he would say to me. *Just breathe, Puddin'.*

Nightly secures my hand in his, slowly moving toward the exit. "Why don't we go to my place? It'll be quieter than going out, and I wouldn't mind a quiet evening with you."

I nod, letting out a tight breath. "Yeah, okay. Sounds good." And it does. It sounds peaceful and far better than being in public, where everyone will feel they have a right to Nightly's time and attention. I'm not up to sharing at the moment.

NIGHTLY

Tension waves off her like heat from a radiator. I try to engage her in conversation on the ride to my place, but after a few one-to-two-word answers, I let her be. With her hand resting in mine, I drive us home.

Home. Maybe someday it'll be ours. It feels rather far off right now. I'm just trying to get us through the evening without her running off. I know I can catch her if she tries, if she insists on me taking a stronger stance. I'm going for patient and understanding and not caveman tracking down his woman. Not to say the second option isn't tempting.

Claim her, my inner beast growls.

She doesn't make a sound until I guide her from the garage and into the house, stopping in the grand living space. Trying to see it from her perspective, wall-to-wall windows with a view of the lit pool and pool house beyond, with the silhouetted mountains barely visible in the moonlight framing it all. I forget how beautiful the view is. I lead her to the couch, stopping short of pushing her down, and release her hand.

"Make yourself at home. I'm just going to drop my bag in the laundry room and then start dinner. You want something to drink?"

She tears her eyes off the wall of windows to find mine. "Wine if you have it. Water if not."

"Red or white?"

She shakes her head. "Whatever you're having."

"Red then."

She nods again, still wide-eyed, scanning the large sitting area full of oversized couches, chairs, and recliners. I'm a big guy, and I have big friends.

"TV or music?" I grab the home control tablet from the coffee table, waiting for her answer.

"Whatever you want."

On a sigh, I set it down, stopping in front of her. I gently grip her chin, garnering her attention. "Do you want to go home?" I don't want to keep her where she doesn't feel comfortable.

"No," seems to pop out of her mouth before she can stop it.

I smile at that, studying her face as she takes me in. This woman who can physically take me down with a few well-placed moves is showing me a different side. Her vulnerability has me wanting to tuck her into my chest and hold her until she's steady. But I don't know if she's open to that. So instead, I kiss her forehead. "Make yourself at home. I'll be right back."

Forgoing TV or music, I pick up my bag I dropped as we walked in and carry it to the laundry room. I set it on the washer and unzip it, letting it air out. I'll tackle washing later or tomorrow, depending on how the evening progresses.

I turn and stop in my tracks. Emmeline is standing in the doorway, uncertainty playing across her beautiful face, turning her golden eyes shiny. I don't address it. I simply take her hand and head to the kitchen.

With her situated at the kitchen bar, I pull out the fixings for breakfast. I know she likes it—seemed like a safe bet. Plus, I've been working on a surprise, hoping for a chance to cook for her.

I'm halfway through the preparation when she finally speaks, starting the conversation instead of barely participating. "I am not easy." She sighs in resignation as if I'd give up based on those four words or any part of her she's shown me thus far.

Not happening.

"I am not looking for easy." I set down my knife, giving her my full attention.

"I don't know how to do this." Her eyes earnestly lock on mine.

"This?" I move closer. Seems like too serious a conversation to have a counter between us.

She motions between us. "I know one-night stands. I don't know how to do more. *Be* more."

I take her hand, kissing her palm, holding it against my chest. "Neither do I, Em. But I'd really like to try with you." Unable to resist any longer, I lean in and press my mouth to hers. Warmth explodes, and she gasps, giving me just enough to capture her bottom lip, teasing with tongue, and another press before pulling back. "Give us a chance."

She follows me, returning my kiss with one of her own. Heated, with far more tongue and needy hands. "Okay," she sighs into our kiss. "This is me giving us a chance."

I devour her mouth. No more holding back.

CHAPTER 14

EMMELINE

I *KNOW* I'VE BEEN KISSED BEFORE. HAD SOME PRETTY darned amazing kisses, I was pretty sure. But this right here—kissing Nightly—seems like a totally different creature entirely. Everyone and everything I've known falls by the wayside. It's only his mouth on mine, his heated body pressed to mine, secured between my thighs as I sit on his barstool and wrap my legs around him, trying to pull him endlessly closer. His smell, his taste, his breathing, competing for air versus devouring is everything I've never known and then some.

"Fuck," he groans against my lips. "This fucking mouth." Gentle, tender Nightly has been unleashed, and I'm the lucky recipient of growly, demanding, hard-as-stone Nightly. I love this Nightly so much.

No… not love.

He ends the marathon of a kiss and steps back. "Jesus." He runs his hand over his mouth and through his hair. "Food. We need food."

"No." I grip his Henley and yank him back to me. "Food later."

"Fuck." His blown pupils ravage every inch of me, scorching with just a look. "Slow." He grips my wrists, forcing my hands to release him. "Food. First," he rumbles against my lips. "I'm starving and not just for you."

"You said first." I lean back, holding up my hands in surrender. "That better mean I'm second."

His runs his lips along my neck, sending shivers down my spine to puddle between my legs. "Promise." Reluctantly, he pulls away and resumes making breakfast for dinner.

NIGHTLY

The twentieth moan around her bite of Dutch baby is all I can take. I stand, my fork clattering to the table. I don't even bother picking it up. "Have you had enough?"

She pushes her plate aside. "God, yes," she breathlessly replies, rising to her feet.

I lift her by the thighs, and she quickly wraps her long legs around me. I squeeze her ass, nuzzling into her neck. "Tell me you want this."

"This?" She grips the back of my hair, tugging till our eyes connect. "Say it."

Damn, that's hot. My girl's found her power, her brave. Her throaty reply has me growing impossibly harder. "Tell me you want me to fuck you."

She shudders, wrapping her arms around my neck. "Yes, I've wanted you since the first day I dropped that stupid note in your bag."

"But that was for a hook-up." It's my turn to grip her hair, ensuring she stays focused on my words. "This is not that. Tell me you understand. *This* is a beginning." I can't take things deeper if she still thinks this is a pump-and-dump kinda situation. I want more.

"This is a beginning," she whispers, tenderness and uncertainty coming forth, feeding my need to take care of her.

"I've got you, Em. We're in this together." Whatever *this* ends up being, which I hope is everything, I'm here for it.

"Together." She presses her mouth to mine, and just as quickly we're on the move.

With no pretext of stringing this out, I set her on her feet before my bed, kissing every inch of skin I can see as I start to undress her. I grip her shirt, pausing. "One of these days, I'm going to fuck you in my jersey. My real one, not one of these imitations sold in the gift store."

She laughs. "Don't tell Bennett. He paid top dollar for these."

"I'll pay him back." I toss her jersey over her head and get lost in the sight of her full breasts held hostage by a sexy black lace bra. "Do your panties match?"

She shrugs, tugging at my own shirt. "Off," she barks. "And who says I'm wearing panties?"

My chest rumbles at the idea of her sitting at my game, among strangers, bare. Granted, she's wearing jeans, but still. "Prove it." I rip off my shirt, toe off my shoes and quickly discard my socks. "Too many fucking clothes," I grouse, hating the sight of her bra and jeans covering what's mine.

Yet even as I complain, the vision of her shimmying out of her jeans, hips swaying side to side is enough to make me drop to my knees, helping the last few inches, kissing down her stomach and inner thigh, glaring at her scant black panties. "Liar."

"Maybe next time." She grips my hair, tilting my head back. "Pants off now."

"Not yet." I remove her shoes, socks and toss them aside with her jeans. "Now, about these panties." I run my nose along her seam, breathing her in, and groan from the unmistakable scent of her arousal. "I need a taste." I grip her ass, kneading, delving lower, pulling on the back of her thong till it pulls tight between her lips, and licking along one side and then the other.

Her grip on my hair tightens on a moan, and I sit back, taking her in with her head tilted as she sways, using my hair and shoulder for support. "Take your bra off. Let me see those gorgeous tits."

She reaches behind her as I grip the sides of her panties and tug them down her long, luscious legs I can't wait to have wrapped around me as I drill into her, finding her pleasure and mine.

I don't know what I expected, but the sight of her landing strip, guiding me to the promised land would have brought me to my knees if I wasn't already bowing at her feet, ready to worship, singing her praises with my mouth, fingers, and cock.

The first swipe of her clit has her calling my name, "Nightly!"

"What do you think of calling me Carter?" Probably not the time, but the idea of her coming with my real name on her lips has my cock throbbing to make it happen.

She bends forward, capturing my face with a tenderness she's never shown before. "Your real name. Carter…" she presses my name into my mouth as it rides on her tongue. "Carter." Stronger this time. I run my fingers along her core, relishing her wetness and slip inside her. She stands, face tilted up. "Carter," she gasps on a tremble. "Please. More."

If I wasn't holding her, I'm pretty sure she'd crumble in my arms as I add a finger and lap at her hard clit, tasting her tartness and savoring her wetness coating my mouth. Slipping in and out of her, finger-fucking her slow and steady, following the rhythm of her hips and the death grip on my hair and head, I kiss her most intimate lips. I drink her juices and hold her as she cries out, mumbling, panting, grinding my name into all of eternity and cementing herself in my soul, filling the hole in my chest to near capacity.

I've wanted her since spotting her behind the counter at Lotti's. It's been a long time coming. Weeks of running, talking, flirting, showing her I want more than a fast fuck.

Her hands on me, gripping, guiding, cajoling are what fantasies are made of. Her need is palpable, heavy in the air, on her tongue, and in every sway of her hips. This right here is what life is all about. The love, the pleasure, the gift of a woman surrendering herself over so completely without reservations or inhibitions.

I suck harder, stroke deeper, knead her flesh as her pleasure ripples across her skin in the form of goosebumps. It's seconds before she clenches around me, squeezing, soaking my fingers and face, calling my name, "Carter!" over and over as she comes, and comes, and comes.

CHAPTER 15

EMMELINE

BEFORE I COME BACK TO MYSELF, I'M FLOATING, panting, and saying his name, "Carter," on endless repeat. He asked me to call him by his given name. A name hardly anyone calls him. It feels like an honor, a moment of true honesty from a man who relishes connection and truth.

Nightly is his hockey façade. Still him, but also a name everyone in the world calls him. I've yet to hear a news anchor, reporter, or announcer call him only Carter. It's always Nightly or Carter "Nightly" McNight. A play on his last name but also a nod to his reputation for being gallant, noble, chivalrous, and kind.

A true leader among men on the ice and off. A knight.

Opening my eyes, I find myself on his bed, splayed out with Carter nuzzling my neck, kissing down my collarbone, one side to the other and then down, down between my breasts, and then lapping, teasing one nipple then the other, sending zaps of pleasure to my clit and back. Arching into his touch, I cry out as he sucks one deep, his fingers sliding in and out of me torturously slow, building me up, curling my toes, reaching, and craving for more. I drag his mouth to mine, needing his mouth on mine, and moan when I find me on his tongue, his face coated with my very essence. And it only makes me hotter for him—all of him.

"Fuck me," I plead, gripping at his jean-clad ass, trying to push them off.

"I need you to come again, baby." He's back to my nipples, tugging and nipping before sucking. "Can you do that for me?" The arousal in his voice hardens my nipples to painful peaks. He hits a magic spot inside, making my legs shake. "Fuck, that's it."

"Oh… God… Carter." I squeeze his fingers, ramming my hips forward and back, taking him deeper, trying to replicate that feeling. "Please."

"I got you, Em." He does that move again, and a full-body spasm has me soaking his bed.

Jesus, I should be embarrassed. I don't know what's he's done to me, what he's unleashed, but I can't turn it off. I don't *want* to turn it off.

He growls, eating up my mouth, sucking hard, devouring my tongue, fucking me with his fingers, hitting that spot over and over again. "Come, baby. Soak me again."

I nearly bend in half. Only his body holds me in place. Crying out, I see stars as I come in an explosion starting in my toes and tingling up my legs to my core, igniting and bursting with such force, I forget how to breathe.

NIGHTLY

"Carter, please." Her pleading does me in. Her second orgasm is even more spectacular than her first. And my name on her lips is everything.

Reluctantly, I pull away, ditch my jeans and boxer briefs. Her eyes never leave me as I grab a condom from the nightstand.

I kneel between her legs, her thighs wet with her arousal. She's fucking soaked my bed, and I've never been more proud or honored. I don't know if this is how she always is, but damn, it's an ego boost feeling her come so hard she drenches my face, my hand, and my sheets.

I knead her breasts, tweaking her nipples between my thumbs and forefingers, flexing my hips so I slip between her pussy lips, coating my condom-covered cock in her wetness. "You sure, Em?" I need her words one more time. "This is a beginning. You understand?"

"Yes, fuck." She clenches her legs around me, trying to draw me into where she needs me, where I need to be. "I know. This the beginning of us. Not a hook-up." She tightens again, raising her hips. "I need your cock, Carter. Stop teasing."

"Not teasing, baby. I want us on the same page." I adjust, so on my next forward slide, the tip of my cock hits her opening. I clench my jaw, bracing my hands on either side of her, and slide home on a growl matched by her returning moan and arch of her neck.

"Fuck. You're so wet and tight." Her pulsing around my cock with each flex of her hips steals my sanity. It's all I can feel. She's everywhere. Her softness, her arms and legs wrapped around me like a cocoon, drawing me in and in and in.

Settling over her, our lips meet in a ravenous kiss full of teeth, tongue, and the taste of us, her pleasure, my desire. I fuck her mouth with languid strokes in equal measure to my cock.

Slow and easy, making it last, drawing her pleasure out, feeling her tense and pull, her body yearning for more—for me.

"Baby," I sigh into our kiss. My heart, my soul, my DNA at a molecular level will never be the same. She's changing me with every stroke, every warm squeeze of her pussy. Her panting breaths, needful pleas, mix with my need to hammer home, fill her up, and mark her as mine from here to eternity, over and over until there is no knowing where she ends and I begin, just her and me… one.

"Carter, please," she pleads, growing desperate, vibrating with the need to come, and I'm more than ready to take it, to feel it, to let her steal my cum with her pleasure.

"You ready, beautiful?"

"Yes, please." She begs so pretty, but she never has to.

I drill in, grinding and pumping, harder, deeper, steady until I hear that sigh, the catch in her breathing, letting me know I found her spot deep inside, my cock nailing it over and over, and my hips grinding me against her clit. Right there. It tingles in my balls, up my back as she clenches and squeezes, pleading in my ear, "Carter. Fuck, right there."

"Yeah, baby. Right. Fucking. There." I punctuate each thrust, pinch her nipples and steal her cries with a kiss.

More and more, higher and higher, deeper, tighter, thrust after thrust until she falls apart, screaming my name, taking her pleasure and forcing mine out of me with each clench of her pussy and quake of her moanful pleas. I surge and surge, pulsing, filling her, breathing her in, and holding her tight.

I thought I knew what sex was. I thought I'd had amazing, mind-blowing orgasms. I thought I'd *given* mind-blowing orgasms. I couldn't have been more wrong. This right here, whatever it is between us is alive, electric, prophesy-worthy, life-affirming,#lifegoals,#mine,#soulmate,#letmecatchmybreathand wearedoingthatagain.

Quickly disposing of the condom, I pull her into my chest, kissing her stupid, telling her how amazing she is, and I'm pretty sure I saw the face of God Herself.

Quietly, tenderly, rapturously, we drift to sleep in each other's arms, and I've never felt such peace and belonging.

CHAPTER 16

EMMELINE

I JERK AWAKE, THE SENSE THAT SOMETHING IS wrong hitting me before I realize my watch is vibrating. I blink at the screen, taking a moment to focus and clear the brain fog of my sex-induced coma.

"Bennett," I whisper into the darkness. Bennett's in trouble.

Then it hits me. *Shit. I'm not home. I'm too far away.*

Jumping out of bed, hardly considering the sleeping giant next to me, I'm hit by the pang of regret. *I'm too far away.*

On automatic, I rush to the bathroom, do my business, splash water on my face, pausing for a second when Nightly's dazed form comes into view in the doorway.

"What's going on? Why are you up?" He brushes his hand across his face. "I can feel you panicking from here."

This man is far too perceptive. "I have to go." I push past him in search of my clothes.

A moment later, soft light fills the space, Nightly having turned on the nightstand lamp. "Here." He hands me my jeans with a quick kiss to my brow. "Tell me what's going on."

I slip on my socks before jamming my legs in my jeans and

pulling them up. "It's Bennett. He—" My watch goes off again. "He needs me." My heart races. *I'm coming, B.*

"Okay." Carter starts pulling on his own clothes.

I don't even question him. He'll get me home quicker than an Uber. This will teach me to not be without my car—or maybe more pointedly, I never should've stayed over. Selfish. Selfish. Selfish.

Bennett never… I stop the thought in its track. He would have. He *has*. B's not a saint. He's not celibate.

Still, the guilt rides me hard as I follow Nightly through his house, grabbing my purse, compulsively checking my phone after settling into his car.

NIGHTLY

After programming Bennett's address into my phone's map app, the ride is silent. It's beginning to feel like this might be her norm. I hear a sniffle seconds before her phone rings, and I consider this is not a normal situation we're dealing with. Something is wrong. I don't push. She's worried. Something is up with Bennett.

She quickly answers her phone, "B, I'm coming." The anguish in her voice undoes me.

"Em." I manage to hear Bennett's emotional rasp. "You don't—"

"I'm switching to video, okay? I need to see your face."

"Yeah, okay."

A moment later, Bennett's sleepy face comes on the screen. I only look for a second, but it's clear he's been crying. I take a deep breath and focus on the road, on getting us to him safely. Needing to offer some form of comfort, I reach across the center console and place my hand on her thigh.

She wipes at her own tears before placing her hand on mine, saying, "We're ten minutes out. Just breathe with me."

Their conversation is a mix of him crying and her comforting, or her crying and him apologizing for dragging her out at this time of morning. It's 2:23 a.m. to be precise. I think we only managed a few hours of sleep, and by the throbbing in my skull, I'm going to need more. But first, I need to get my girl to her best friend.

EMMELINE

"We're here," I practically shout into the phone. I'm out the car as soon as Nightly parks, rushing to Bennett's door, entering my code into his keyless entry pad. It unlocks, and I'm rushing through, ending the call and dumping my phone and purse at the entry table. "I'm here!" I kick off my shoes and dash down the hall to his room.

Nightly's footfall is not far behind, but I can't stop to explain. I can only be grateful he got me here so quickly, didn't make it about himself on the ride here, and hasn't dumped me and left. I know this is screwed up, but now's not the time to figure out mine and Bennett's codependency issues.

When I throw open Bennett's door, the light from the hall catches his teary gaze. "Em." He opens his arms to me, and I practically dive for him on his bed, falling over him to his other side.

"I'm here."

"I'm sorry." He has the nerve to try and apologize for needing me as though I haven't called him like this before.

"I'm sorry I took so long to—"

He crushes me to his chest, burying his face in my neck. "You're here now."

"I'm here. You're safe. We left that place a long time ago. It can't hurt you anymore. It's just a memory. It can't hurt you." I catch a steady breath and ask, "What do you know?"

"I'm home in my bed. I'm not there."

"What else."

"You're here, and you're trembling. Em?"

"I'm okay. I was just scared because I wasn't here, B." I can't stop the sob. I wasn't here.

A warm hand lands on my back. It's not B's. His are still wrapped around me. "You're here, baby. You made it. Please don't cry." Nightly's calming touch and tender voice laced with concern ease my guilt. I'm here. Bennett is okay. I'm here.

"Shh." Bennett's breath tickles my ear. Slowly, he moves over, dragging me with him, closer to his side of the bed so I'm in the middle. "You might as well join us. I'm not ready to let her go just yet, and I imagine you aren't either."

"B," I breathe, unable to voice my shock he's letting Nightly in, and even more surprising, Nightly's not putting up a fit demanding I get out of another man's bed only hours after being in his and sharing something so remarkable it brings more tears to my eyes and renewed sobs.

"It's okay, Em." Nightly kisses my neck seconds before pressing in behind my back, freeing the covers from under me. He scoots forward, and I'm fully tucked into his chest, wrapped between him and Bennett. My twin-soul in front of me and my someone pretty darn special behind me. How am I this lucky? Peace I've never known filters through my bloodstream. I'm supposed to be comforting Bennett, and yet between these two, I've never felt so cherished or understood.

We all take a collective breath and slowly relax into the warmth and comfort of not having to face our demons alone.

I wake to find Bennett still sound asleep facing me, and Nightly wrapped around me from behind. We've barely moved. My heart pings, and my eyes mist when I spot my hand in Bennett's on the bed between us, with Nightly's larger hand covering ours. He's adding the protective layer, ensuring we *feel* and *stay* safe, sequestered in his hold.

Ensuring *we* feel safe.

This man is determined to undo me, knock down every wall I've built around my heart, not by force, but by tender, gentle, selfless acts of kindness.

My heart aches at the idea of not having nights like I had with Nightly last night before Bennett's PTSD nightmare. Though we said it, it definitely felt like the start of something remarkable. *Start* isn't even accurate, more like we cemented our connection that has only grown since we met. Now, here I am in bed with my bestie because he needed me, *and* the guy who's working hard to own my softening heart.

How does this work? How many times will Nightly jump in before resentment or jealousy appears? How do I honor my friendship with Bennett and not leave him behind while forging something new and strong with Nightly?

It's not only about Bennett's needs, but mine too. I need B as much as he needs me, just in different ways. I don't have nightmares, at least not usually, and not about my time in service. I have social anxiety, particularly in large crowds. I have an overall leeriness of men. I have survivor's guilt and an overarching weight of unworthiness. I don't like stepping out of my comfort zone. And Bennett *is* my comfort zone—has been for years.

Doubt looming in my head, I slowly extract myself from their hold, in need of a shower and a toothbrush.

CHAPTER 17

NIGHTLY

WAKING UP ALONE IN ANOTHER MAN'S BED THAT smells of my girl and him is not exactly how I thought my night would end, or how my morning would begin. After pulling on the jeans I tossed off in the middle of night when I got hot, I go in search of another bathroom since someone is in Bennett's ensuite shower. I find a hall bath, take a leak and finger-brush my teeth with the toothpaste I found in a drawer. It'll have to do for now.

Heading the way we entered last night, I stretch out my sore muscles from my game, which seems further away than just last night. The smell of coffee and bacon finds me in the kitchen, staring at a shirtless Bennett in sweatpants and a huge mug of coffee. The first thing that strikes me is how fit he is. The second, how tired he looks. I can relate.

"Morning." He holds up his cup. "Want one?"

"Yes, please. Could I get it in an IV drip?"

He chuckles and then winces like his head hurts. He probably has an emotional hangover. "I can only offer it in liquid form. What you do with it is between you and God."

"Fair enough." I doctor my coffee with sugar and creamer and eye him as I take my first sip. "You doing okay?"

He shrugs. "Better than I thought I'd be."

"Good. I'm sorry she wasn't—" I start.

"I'm sorry for messing up your night," he interjects.

"You didn't mess up our night." Running my fingers through my hair, I smile at the memory of last night before his… episode. "We had a great night. You only interrupted our sleep." I yawn.

"No, I really am sorry. I tried not to call… but… the panic… I couldn't…"

I grip his shoulder before I even consider he might not be okay with my touch. When he leans in, I set down my mug and his and pull him into a hug. "It's okay, man." Him fisting my shirt as he hugs me back has me hugging him tighter. "It's okay. We've got you." Seconds turn into minutes before he loosens his grip.

Taking his lead, I release him and step back. "There's just one thing I need to know. Man-to-man."

He nods.

"Do you want her? Do you love her? Am *I* stepping between something here?" I don't really want the answer, but I need it. I've no desire to come between what they have, especially if he's in love with her, and she's just never seen it.

He hands me my coffee before grabbing his. "No. I mean, we're complicated. But no, I'm not in love with her, and she's not in love with me. We've never… we aren't like that. It's not sexual." He shrugs again, his eyes watering, chin quivering. "It's survival."

I grip the back of his neck, garnering his eyes, needing him to hear me. "It's okay. I'm not taking her from you—I understand you're kind of a package deal. We'll figure it out. You come hang with us, or we hang here. We got you."

"Um…" We turn to find a teary-eyed Em, staring like she doesn't know what she just walked in on, but she's not mad about it.

"Morning, beautiful." I release Bennett and kiss her shower-warmed lips, wanting more but only stealing a taste.

"Good morning, you two." She pats my chest. "I see you started the good stuff without me."

"Never." Bennett hands her a mug that matches his, smiling. "Hot and sugary, just the way you like it."

Their level of friendship is endearing, and if I were a weaker man, intimidating. He knows her deep down to her core, and I've just started to get to know her. But I can't deny what they have is enviable. And I'd never ask her to give up someone who takes such good care of her. I may not yet fully understand their relationship or what they've been through together and apart, but I've no intention of becoming a wedge between them. Maybe just a corner to round out their circle into more of a triangle.

"Thanks." She tentatively sips, her gaze bouncing between the two of us.

"Breakfast will be ready in thirty." His returning stare with his best friend—my girl—seems knowing.

She steps into him, laying her head on his chest. "You doing okay?"

"Yeah, Puddin'. I'm good. Don't—"

"I'm sorry—"

"—you dare apologize for having a life," he finishes before she can complete the apology I feel just as deeply. He needed her, and she was with me. *I'm* conflicted. She has to be as well.

Smiling up at him, studying his tired eyes, she bops his nose, and he laughs. "I have thirty minutes?"

"You can have thirty-*five*, but not a second longer."

She hands him her coffee. "Keep it warm for me."

"Of course." He meets my confused look. "I'll make a new pot. See you in a bit."

"What—"

Em grabs my hand. "You heard him. We have thirty. Come on." She tugs me out the front door, but not before Bennett lifts my cup from my hands, smiling like he knows what's happening.

"Where are we going?" I don't fight her, but we're both barefoot and have zero belongings, no wallet, phones, or keys.

"Trust me," is all she says as we make our way across Bennett's yard to the house next door with the same security setup with keyless entry. After she punches in a code, the door unlocks, and she tugs me inside before closing and locking it behind us. "Welcome to my home."

I relax on a laugh. "Of course you live next door."

She only bats her eyes at me. "Where else would I live?"

"Honestly, I'm kinda surprised you don't live together."

"No." She shimmies out of her pants, leaving them where they drop, and continues tugging me down a hall. I barely take in my surroundings, given her incredible legs are on full display. "Momma needs her space."

"Momma?" I could take this so many directions. "Wait. What are you wearing?"

"We have clothes stashed at each other's places. It's convenient." She releases me once we're in what must be her bedroom.

It's far more feminine than I would have imagined. Purples and pinks with touches of green and white, totally girly, and it makes me smile, discovering this piece of her. She likes purple and pink flowers, soft and comfortable, and the air is coated in her scent: roses and vanilla.

"I'm gonna need you naked for this next part." She lifts her shirt, and I nearly choke to find her naked.

"Where the fuck are your underthings?" I growl, catching her by the waist.

"I didn't wear any. Told you *maybe next time*." She smirks, tipping her chin in challenge.

My sexy-as-fuck woman. I want to swat her ass, but my hardening cock has other ideas. Though spanking could be hot too.

"What next part?" Not five minutes ago, she was near tears finding me and her best friend having a rather raw and important conversation. We should discuss it. Be sure she's okay with what all transpired.

"The part where I ride your cock because you've got me all hot and bothered being kind and gentle toward my bestie. Most men would be threatened. But not you—" She pats my chest, right over my heart. "You have a heart-to-heart and come up with a *we. We got him*—you said."

"Em." The moisture on her lashes and the awe in her eyes do me in. "Baby, please don't cry. You're killing me." I press my mouth to hers, giving me a second to savor this moment with her.

"I don't for one second pretend to understand what you two have been through. The fact you're both here, unharmed, at least not catastrophically, is enough for me. He's important to you. You love each other. As long as it's not romantically crossing any lines—I'm all in. And if that means he's a part of our life, maybe more than I anticipated—I'm okay with it."

She closes the distance, taking the next kiss for herself, and I let her. "This mouth. The things you say," she groans across my lips. "I need you naked. Now."

Done. She doesn't have to ask me twice. As I strip, she pulls the covers back on her bed, then rummages through her nightstand. "I don't suppose you have a condom?"

CHAPTER 18

NIGHTLY

"I DON'T." THE REALITY OF OUR SITUATION DOESN'T dissuade me. Wrapping my arms around her from behind, I kiss her neck. "There are other things we can do." Gentle suck behind her ear. "I wouldn't mind a little snack before breakfast."

She shivers, and the nipple under my palm hardens. I squeeze and tweak it as my other hand travels between her legs. Or I could just bend her over, right here, and fuck the sleepy emotions from her voice, replaced with hoarseness from her screams of pleasure.

"Or we could forgo the condom." She twists in my hold, lifting to her tippy-toes. I grip her ass and hold her against me as she fits a leg around my hip, grinding against me, dragging her wet pussy along my balls and the base of my saluting cock.

"Fuck, Em," I moan against her lips, wanting her so damn much.

"I'm on birth control, and it's been a long while for me and never without a condom. I'm good, cleared every test."

"Same. But if we go bare, we won't be going back. You're tempting the beast." Another shiver and I'm hoisting her up; her legs wrap around me on a gasp as I fit perfectly between her thighs where our most intimate places meet. "Are we doing this?"

Please have brain cells enough to consent, for I'm sorely lacking blood in my brain at the moment.

"I need you on the bed so I can ride this beautiful cock." Her grinding against me has me squeezing her ass and guiding my finger through her wet folds from behind, slipping a finger inside her.

"Or you ride me just like this until you come." She swivels her hips, riding my finger. I add another and swallow her moan with a kiss. "Then I bend you over and fuck you like the greedy girl you are over this sweet, flowery comforter."

"Gah, this mouth." Her cunt squeezes my fingers, drawing dueling groans from us. "I want it all, Carter." She increases her pace, panting, "Give it to me."

Jesus, this woman. Born to ride my fingers, my cock, my face. She fits me perfectly. "Can you come like this?"

"I'm—" Her strong legs and hips guide her up and down my fingers, her clit rubbing against my abs, soaking me.

"So fucking perfect. So damn beautiful, taking what you need, what you want." I kiss along her jaw and down her neck, eating up the ecstasy riding her face as she rides my fingers. "Gonna fuck you so good, baby."

"Carter," she gasps.

"Hard and deep." I bite the top of her breast, trying to reach her nipple, tearing more moans from her sweet throat. "You're gonna drench me aren't you, Em? You're gonna come so hard your juices flood over my fingers and cock."

"Fuck. I'm… please, Carter." She's delirious with the build, muscles tensing, her entire body undulating against me.

"This sweet pussy is my salvation, Em." I suck her earlobe. "You hear me?"

"Yes. Please…" The way she begs is a siren song to my cock.

"You want my cock, baby? You need it?"

"Yes!" She grips the back of my hair, tilting my head, her lips grazing mine.

"Then you fucking come," I growl across her lips, delving in and stealing a kiss as she shatters, soaking my fingers, my abdomen, my cock. Squeezing my hand so damn good, I'm groaning with her as she comes, quaking, shaking, and whimpering my name as an edict, locking her in place in my heart, my life, my bed.

Slowly, my woman relaxes, resting her head on my shoulder. "You've killed me," she mumbles, tickling the hairs along my neck.

"That's all you, beautiful." I gently pull out of her, holding her angst me, relishing her laxed, tender state.

"I think I could come just from your dirty talk."

I chuckle and knead her ass. "Speaking of—" I run my fingers along her soaked pussy. "Can you take more?"

"You promised me your cock," she pouts.

I hide my smile in her neck, kissing her there. "I did, and I'm desperate for you."

EMMELINE

On a groan, I extract myself from around Carter. He holds me close, his cock rubbing along my body as my feet land on steady ground. "I want to taste you," falls from my lips before I consider what that means for me. I haven't done that in a really, really long time. It's a boundary we'll need to unearth another time.

He cups my cheek, kissing me softly. "Not this time." I'm not sure if he sees the relief in my eyes, but he brushes his hand along my jaw, then his lips meet mine in a tender joining that quickly grows to feasting. My body responds like I didn't just have an incredible orgasm, like my limbs aren't weak and sore, barely able to move.

Breaking our kiss, he pats my ass and motions to the bed. "On all fours, facing the window."

I hesitate only for a second. I'd come to my house with every intention of riding him, but the idea of him riding me has my pussy throbbing with the need to be filled so completely by him, be surrounded by him, devoured by him.

On my knees and hands, I glance back, wiggling my ass to tease the beast he keeps teasing me with. "Times a-wasting. Breakfast will be cold if you don't hurry."

His smirk is inciting, thrilling me that I can be playful with him. I've never been a particularly playful person in bed. He brings it out of me.

"Taking a moment to enjoy the view." He kisses along my spine, and his hands follow, caressing, kneading, slipping between my legs to finger my clit, and I jolt. "Too sensitive?"

"No. Just… maybe a little," I admit.

"What about here?" He trails his fingers along my slit, spreading me, dipping inside and out. Teasing. Spreading my moisture up to my ass, rounding my asshole.

"No!" Lurching, my hips dart away before I can school my reaction on a tight gasp.

"Shit." His hands leave my body, and he steps back.

Coldness overtakes me, and I shiver in the absence of his touch. I curl into myself. "I'm sorry—"

Oh, shit. What have I done? No. No. No. Nightly's different. He's not *him*.

"Don't apologize." The bed dips, and Nightly carefully guides my face to his. "Did someone hurt you, Em? Take what is only yours to give?"

Denial is on the tip of my tongue, but before I can protest, he pulls me into his arms. "It's okay. You don't have to tell me. Just maybe give me a roadmap so I don't walk us into a minefield."

I bury my face in his neck as he adjusts us to the top of my bed and pulls the covers over me. I take a moment to feel his arms around me. His deep breathing. The rhythm of his heart beating against me. I'm safe. He'll never hurt me. "It wasn't intentional. Sometimes I forget I have… damage when I'm with you."

He kisses the top of my head, running his hand along my back. "I'm glad you feel safe with me." He tips my chin. "Do you want to talk about it?"

"I guess we should, but maybe not now. Bennett—"

"Is waiting on us," he finishes.

I peek up at him, trying to gauge what he's feeling. "I'm starving. But you didn't—" I wiggle in his lap.

A tight grip on my hip stills me. "Now you're being cruel." He jokes. "Don't make me hard again when I have to face your best friend over food."

I extricate myself from his lap, saying, "I'm sorry I ruined the mood."

He stands and wraps me in a hug. "You didn't ruin anything." He presses a kiss to my forehead. "But I need you to wear underthings when we go back over there, or I won't be able to focus."

"I can do that." After kissing his cheek, I pull out of his embrace and walk to my closet for *underthings* and clean clothes, and toss over my shoulder, "Bennett has clothes in the guest room if you want something more comfortable than jeans."

A quick shower to clean up, fresh clothes, my hair in a messy bun and Nightly in one of Bennett's t-shirts and black joggers, we return to his house for breakfast.

I'm worried about the discussion to come, yet feel lighter for having breached the topic of my own trauma. Bennett isn't the only one with issues, further tying us to one another.

CHAPTER 19

EMMELINE

WE FIND BENNETT IN THE KITCHEN, PLATING breakfast with loaded eggs, full of ham and apparently every vegetable he had in the refrigerator; bacon; home fries; and biscuits. "B, this is a feast."

"It's a good thing I know thirty minutes for you never means thirty minutes. Plus, I had a head start." He loads us up with dishes to take to the table. "Though, you really weren't gone that long." He frowns, silently asking if everything is okay.

"Yeah, Nightly hit a trip wire." I sit, asking, "Who wants juice?" readying to fill our glasses, but when no one responds, I look up to find them frozen in place, Nightly staring at me, worry furrowing his brow, and Bennett glancing between the two of us. "What?"

"I'd rather we didn't discuss that now, seems better suited for a you-and-me conversation." With a clenched jaw, Nightly sits to my left, replying, "I'll have juice... please."

"B?" I prompt, ignoring the awkward elephant I dumped in the room.

"Same." He takes the seat across from me, eyes drilling into mine. "You're going to scare him off if he believes you can't have any serious conversations without me around."

The echo of my heartbeat resonates in my head as panic builds. We haven't even had a real date, and I'm fucking everything up already. First, I freak out when he touches me intimately with only a desire for pleasure, and I'm triggered by old trauma, killing the mood. Then, I cross the line, sharing something that should have remained between us, forgetting Nightly doesn't truly know the depth of our dependency or that I don't have many boundaries with Bennett.

Nightly rests his hand on my leg, his tender gaze solely focused on me. "Do you need him around for this conversation, *not* about our… intimacy, but about your past?"

His touch is a balm to my racing thoughts and panic. I glance at Bennett, waiting for any indication of how he feels about it. Will he feel left out? When I get nothing but his patient gaze, I turn back to Nightly.

"No. You're right. I was being flippant." I sit back, gripping Nightly's hand. "My trauma is not my favorite topic. I was trying to make light of it, but I didn't consider it was also betraying something sideways that happened between you and me in an intimate moment. I shouldn't have brought it up. I thought I was just outing myself, but in fact, I was betraying your trust. What we've shared—what we're building—is important to me. Please don't think otherwise.

"I'm sorry I didn't give you a heads-up on my triggers. And I'm sorry I brought it up in front of Bennett. Please forgive me. I'll work to do better next time." Look at me, adulting, speaking in full sentences, recognizing I was wrong, apologizing.

Gripping the back of my neck, he presses his forehead to mine before pressing his lips against my heated skin. "Forgiven, always. I promise to be more understanding as we navigate what you and I have, and what you and Bennett have."

"I feel like we need a group hug." Bennett's smile is ridiculously huge. "My girl is growing up."

"If I wasn't so hungry, I'd kick your ass," I tease.

"You could try," he goads.

Nightly laughs. "So, right back at it then?"

"Basically." I shrug, reaching across the table to squeeze B's hand. "Thanks for the food. It looks amazing."

"Thanks for saving me last night." Bennett loads his plate, no eye contact. We're moving on. Enough touchy-feely.

Nightly pulls me aside after cleaning up breakfast—the cook doesn't clean. "I need to head home. I have laundry and packing to do."

"Packing?" I hold his hand, running my fingers down his palm before flipping it over and massaging it.

His arm around my back pulls me closer, studying my hands on his. "Yeah, we leave tomorrow for three away games."

"You're leaving town?" I don't hide my disappointment well. It's not the first time he's had away games since we started doing whatever it is we're doing. Yet, I'm sad to see him leave when we just moved our relationship to the next level. I mean, mind-blowing sex. Yes, please. Beyond the amazing, intimate sex, emotionally, we've jumped leaps and bounds. He slept in Bennett's bed with me and Bennett in it too! I know hockey is his job—his passion. I mean, damn, I'm going to miss him.

His smile is knowing as he kisses my nose like he thinks it's sweet. "I was thinking you could pack a bag, spend the day and night with me. I'd like to wake up with you before I leave."

"You sure? I don't want—"

"I'm sure." He circles my waist, pulling me flush against him. "We need to talk about… *things*, but I thought we could watch movies and cook. Just hang. I'm a little tired too. I wouldn't mind a nap, especially if you're in my arms."

"I love naps." I catch the twinkle in his eyes, taking me in as if I'm the one sparkling. It's him. His warmth is infectious. I want to crawl in his lap and stay.

"So, yes then?"

"Yes." I kiss him once, twice, and one more time for good measure. "Let me tell Bennett."

He stops me from pulling away. "He can come, if you want." He sounds sincere.

"Really?" I'm torn between him getting to know my bestie and getting to have alone time—potentially *sexy* alone time—with Carter.

"I'm sure. He can come in a few hours, give us time to talk and figure some things out."

It sounds a bit ominous. But I take his hand and lead him out of the kitchen to find Bennett in his living room. "B, we're heading to Nightly's. He needs to get ready to leave town tomorrow. I'm gonna pack a bag and stay the night. Do you want to come by later, say around three, to watch movies and hang?"

He stands, shoving his hands in his pockets. "I don't want to impose."

"You're not imposing. Bring a bag, stay the night." Nightly motions to his body. "I'll wash your clothes, and you could just wear these if you'd like."

"Thanks. I appreciate the inclusion." The peace that comes over B's face has my feelings for Nightly settling in deeper. I know from experience, he's not ready to be alone for long.

They bro-shake. B gets Nightly's address, and we go to my place so I can pack a bag. I have work tomorrow too.

As I grab clothes, I consider workout gear. "I assume we're not running tomorrow?" I turn to Nightly sitting on my bed.

"No. Sorry. When I get back, we can start up again. But I have a decent home gym with a treadmill if you want to work out there before heading to Lotti's or home—whatever your day looks like."

"I could do that before I head to Raven's Hope, then work the rest of the day at Lotti's." I'll feel better about myself if I don't skip doing some sort of exercise.

"Raven's Hope?" He takes the clothes in my arms and starts packing them in the duffel on my bed.

"It's a shelter and food bank Bennett and I help support with food and donated clothes." I tilt my head, considering. "I actually wanted to talk to you about it. See if maybe you or some of your teammates might like to help out. Joey, the executive director, is a great guy and gives his lifeblood for the place. But he's really hurting. They need funding and volunteers. I thought maybe if you or a few guys came by, it might help get others involved. I don't know. He needs help, and I only have so much money and time to give."

He pulls me between his legs. "Can you take me there when I get back? Maybe after practice one day so we're not rushed? I can properly check it out, meet Joey and go from there?"

I practically fall into him, pressing my forehead to his. "Yes, that would be amazing." I kiss his upturned mouth. "Thank you for considering it."

"You don't need to thank me. The Dragons are always looking for ways to give back. If everything pans out, we can get our PR team involved, get Raven's Hope the publicity it needs. Do some good."

"That would be amazing."

CHAPTER 20

NIGHTLY

HAVING EM IN MY HOME FEELS RIGHT, LIKE SHE was always meant to be here filling the space with her vanilla and roses scent, adding light where there's too much dark, and casting shadows to soften the rough edges. I'm not one to hide from my emotions or back away from difficult situations. I do try to ease conflict, be a voice of reason, find mutual ground to grow connection where there is none. Yet as Em sits on the other end of the couch—too fucking far from me—my lungs seize, and my thoughts torpedo to murdering the walking-dead men who dared lay a hand on her. A crime at any age, but at sixteen, when her life was just beginning and her body not always her own, as she moved from a young girl into womanhood, they took something from her, something that wasn't theirs to take. They took her choice, her confidence, her innocence, marking her in a way I'll never fully understand as a man.

"He pinned me down while his friends watched." She sniffles at the memory, her chin trembling, killing me with each agonizing detail. "The first guy… penetrated me vaginally. The, uh, second guy… went lower."

Sonofabitch. I want to kill them. I asked her to unburden

herself, give me her pain so I can help carry it. Perhaps help heal it. If she can survive the deeds, I can survive hearing about them. But still, knowing they touched her without permission is a hard pill to swallow.

"Please come here," I ask for the third time.

She shakes her head, reaching for a tissue. "I can't have your touch. Not now, not while they're in my head."

Because they're in her head, I want to hold her, erase the memory of their touch. It's selfish of me to still want to comfort her in the only way I know how, with my body wrapped around hers, protecting, soothing.

Honoring her wishes, I stay put, even though everything in me bellows in protest, demanding I eliminate the distance between us.

"There were five of them, but only two… violated me before the police showed up. Someone heard my screams and called 911. I'd never been so thankful to hear sirens in my life."

"Were they arrested?" *Please tell me they're rotting in prison.*

"Two were caught that day. The others were arrested later when the original two confessed and gave them up." She swipes at her tears, giving me a watery smile. "The woman who called 911 recorded them on her phone from her window. She didn't dare come down, but she did the next best thing—she called for help and captured their faces so even if they hadn't turned on each other, they probably would have gotten arrested eventually."

"Are they still in jail?" *Please tell me they are.* I can't have my woman worrying she'll run into them around every corner.

"The two who raped and beat me got life. The others received twenty years for Rape in Concert." Slowly, she stands, stretching, collects her tissues and tosses them away in the kitchen trash.

I follow, wanting to be close in case she changes her mind about comfort. "What happened to you afterwards?"

"I was in the hospital recovering from my injuries. I had a jaw facture, contusions. They weren't gentle. I never stopped fighting." She comes to stand beside me, leaning against the counter. "I started my self-defense training the day after I got out. By the time I joined the Marines two years later, I was pretty fierce but also had a really big chip on my shoulder. Probably not the smartest move, joining the military, where it's mainly men."

"And you met Bennett?"

"I saw B the first day of basic training, we acknowledged each other but didn't really talk until a week later."

"What happened a week later?"

"One of the guys in another class decided I needed a lesson in humility because I was a high performer in my class—surpassing him. He was a big mother, thought he had a better use for my mouth… Again, I fought." Her teary eyes meet mine. "It sucks being a woman sometimes. Even now, trained in self-defense and combat, there are guys bigger and stronger than me, who I'll never be able to best."

Jesus, I can't. I open my arms, and she hesitates only for a second before melting into my chest. I wrap my arms around her, kissing her head, whispering, "I'm sorry, Em. I wish I could take it all way. Tell you there's no more bad guys, but you and I both know that's a lie. Men suck sometimes. I want to protect you, and I will, but I acknowledge the problem is bigger than you or me."

"I know. That's one of the reasons B and I are so close. He's my protector, my rock, and I'm his comfort from his PTSD from service. We're good together, more broken apart."

Thank God for Bennett. "What happened to that guy?"

"Bennett heard him grumbling about me. Kept an eye on

him. Ended up following him, but one of his buddies distracted B long enough for the guy to get ahold of me. When Bennett found me, I was fighting and losing. Bennett provided the distraction I needed to get on my feet and show the guy what happens when you don't ask nicely."

She looks up from my chest. "I broke his nose, jaw, and leg. He was court-martialed, dishonorably discharged, and is serving thirty years for sexual assault."

I don't even try to hide my smile. "My woman's a badass."

She shakes her head. "I don't feel like a badass."

I tap her chin. "A badass survives, learns how to protect herself, stands by her best friend, saves customers from abusive partners, and lets a humbled hockey player in her bed when she has every right to never want a man to touch her ever again."

"Hmm, I like the way you think." On tiptoes, she presses her mouth to mine. I let her lead, more important now than ever. I want her to feel safe and protected with me.

I pull back before she can delve in deeper and sidetrack us. "Can we talk about triggers, no-go areas?"

"Yeah, but can we have a snack? I'm starving. Emotional turmoil really makes me hungry." She tosses me wide smile that shines in her eyes—no tears—and eases my mangled thoughts of all she's been through.

"You're a remarkable woman, Emmeline Weston. Strong. Resilient. Fierce. Yet also kind, generous, and giving." I kiss her forehead and move to the refrigerator to pull out food for lunch. "Do you like tuna fish salad sandwiches?"

"I've never met a sandwich I didn't like."

"Good." I point to the cabinets behind her. "Can you grab me a pan to boil the eggs in?"

"Ooo, can we do a few extra? I love hardboiled eggs."

I kiss the tip of her nose. “Baby, you can have as many as you like. Would you rather have egg salad sandwiches?” I love both. Maybe we make both.

We do both… *and* leave a few hardboiled eggs for later, or tomorrow.

CHAPTER 21

EMMELINE

MY LEGS ARE DRAPED OVER NIGHTLY'S LAP, Bennett on the floor in front of me, all eyes trained on the TV watching our second movie of the day. This is exactly how I love spending a lazy Sunday. If only every day could be like this. Maybe not how it started or all the sexual assault talk. Despite it all, I feel lighter—at peace.

I imagined Nightly would be one of those guys who watches sports twenty-four-seven. He swears he doesn't, *and* he loves movies. I've no reason not to believe him, and the smile on his face and the endless touches—not complaining—seem like he's enjoying himself. Having us in his space is no hardship, which is a relief, as I really like his place. It's huge—a little too big—but it affords him a gated community, keeping fans from following him home, which apparently is a thing. Psycho much?

He even has a guesthouse out back. He calls it a pool house because of the pool, but it's a complete two-bedroom, two-bath, kitchen, living room… home. Hence, guesthouse.

Bennett has been teasing him about moving in there. I keep giving him the stink-eye. *Who's gonna scare off the nice man now?*

Teasing about moving in there when I move in here with Nightly. It's too much, too fast. Though my heart flutters like it's fully on board.

B and I never considered what would happen to the other when, if, we got involved in serious relationships—with other people. In the seven years we've been friends, neither of us has been in a relationship that lasted more than a few weeks. Despite my desire to have a family, my actions have leaned toward casual, avoiding connection at all costs. Case in point, me fighting the connection with Nightly. Plus, he's famous. Though as he lounges on the couch, legs spread, massaging my feet, he seems like any other hotter-than-Hades-guy-next-door. The kind of guy I want to keep, father my children, change diapers with, have endless lazy Sunday naps with, and make forever plans with.

He catches me staring and does a double-take before leaning over, mapping out the details of my face, and licking his lips as he checks out mine. "What are you thinking about?"

"You," pops out too freely. I can't take it back. I don't really want to. It's been a day of truths. Why not add this one too?

"What about me?"

"I like you," I whisper. The importance of those words flickers in the back of my eyes and has my heart pounding.

His brows shoot up before settling into a devastating smile. "I like you too."

"I want to keep you," I admit even softer than before, like if the universe hears, it'll jinx it.

"Okay. Let's do that," he agrees.

"Yeah?"

"Only if I get to keep you too."

Yes, please. "Deal."

"Bennett, I'm gonna need you to avert your eyes for a minute."

Nightly leans in, so close, yet too far. "Let's seal it with a kiss, beautiful."

"Ew, Mommy and Daddy are gonna make out." B pauses the movie and jumps up. "Bathroom break."

The doorbell rings right as Nightly's lips meet mine.

"I'll get it!" Bennett yells.

I don't let it distract me from the man attacking my face. It's only the groceries we ordered to make dinner.

"Come 'ere." Nightly pulls me to him, half lying on me, half sitting, and deepens the kiss. The best kiss, the kind that holds the promise of more—everything.

"Uh, Nightly," Bennett's voice interrupts my thoughts of *more*. "This woman says she belongs to you."

Slowly, we break our kiss, blinking at each other for a second before Bennett's words sink in. "What?"

Nightly jumps to his feet, pulling me with him, ensuring I'm steady with my hand in his as he faces the woman standing next to Bennett. "Willa? What are you doing here?"

A gorgeous woman with red curly hair stares between Nightly, me, and our joined hands. "Seems like you've got your hands full, little brother," she quips seconds before a smile splits her face and she rushes forward to give him a hug.

Sister, I mouth at Bennett. He shrugs like he's not fazed, yet his eyes give him away. He's dazzled by her.

Nightly releases his sister. "Emmeline, I'd like you to meet my big sister, Willa. Willa, this is my girl, Emmeline, and her best friend,

Bennett." He holds me to his side even while Willa leans in for an awkward hug.

"It's nice to meet you," I say, feeling a little embarrassed on how she found us making out on the couch.

"Same." Then she turns to Bennett, giving him a hug. Surprisingly, he hugs her back like it's no hardship. "Best friend, huh?" Barely letting him go, she checks him out.

"Yeah, the best-est." He winks at me.

"If I had a best friend like you, we'd get into so much trouble." She waggles her eyebrows at him.

I swear Bennett blushes.

"Willa, what are you doing here? Are you staying or just passing through?" Nightly pulls me down, reclaiming his seat on the couch with me beside him.

"Staying." She sits on the other couch, patting the seat next to her, urging Bennett to sit. "A few days, if that's okay. I just flew in from Milan. I'm exhausted and want to sleep for twenty-four hours."

"Stay as long as you want. I leave town for three games in the morning." He pulls me closer with his arm around my shoulder. "I'll be back early Friday, like middle of the night."

"I fly out for a few days next week. Then I'm off for a few weeks. I'd like to go to a game or two, if you can swing it."

"Done. I'm hoping Em and Bennett will come to Saturday's game." He looks between us hopefully.

I've got no plans. "Sounds good."

Bennett agrees. By the starstruck look in his eyes, he'd agree to just about anything right now.

"Willa's a pilot," Nightly says.

"I fly mainly charters. But I've been known to do private jets too," she adds.

"Sounds like a cool job." Color me impressed. Besides the military, I've never run into a female pilot.

"What do you do, Emmeline?" Willa's assessing gaze would have intimidated me at one time, but not for many years now.

"I own a coffee shoppe."

"Oh?" She leans forward. "Have I been there, Carter?"

"No. I don't think so—"

"It's Lotti's Latte," Bennett chimes in.

She turns to him. "And you?"

B motions to me. "I'm Em's manager."

"Best friends *and* you work together. Which came first?" Willa sits back, getting more comfortable.

"Friends," I say at the same time Bennett says, "Co-workers."

She laughs, "Friends? Co-workers? Which is it?"

"They met in the Marines and became fast friends—so both are accurate." Nightly kisses my temple.

I smile at his show of affection. The way he jumped off the couch earlier, I was worried he was going to distance himself. Instead, he's drawing me closer, as if to make a statement to his sister. I don't mind him chiming in on Bennett and my history either. Seems like acceptance of B's place in my life—and his too.

"Marines? I was in the Air Force."

"Is that where you learned to fly?" Bennett asks.

"Yes, sir." She winks at him.

I swear he blushes again. I've never seen B blush before today. This is delicious and entirely unexpected. "I think B has a crush," I side-whisper to Nightly.

"I noticed." He doesn't seem too pleased. Then he shrugs. "She's a big girl. Makes her own choices," he whispers back, relaxing into the couch. "You want to stay here or the pool house?" Nightly asks Willa.

"That depends. Are you having wild monkey sex tonight? 'Cause I really don't need to hear all that."

"Pool house it is." Nightly suddenly rises, not even laughing, pulling me behind him. "Food in the fridge if you get hungry."

Wide-eyed, I stare at Bennett, who looks at Nightly. "Um, I think I'll stay in the pool house too then."

"Suit yourself." He stops and turns. "B, can you stay long enough to get the groceries though?"

"Yeah, you okay if I still cook?"

"Make yourself at home. I'll be out later to grab some food too." He turns back to his hallway that'll take us to his room.

"Um, Nightly?" I catch his focus.

He only shakes his head. "Nope. I've shared you all afternoon. I need some alone time before I leave for four days."

I glance at B, who only waves me off, mouthing *I'm good.* "Okay." I can't say I hate the idea.

He waves to his sister and Bennett. "See y'all in the morning or maybe later if you're still around."

"It's nice to meet you," I call back to his sister.

"You too, future-sis-in-law!" she hollers back.

I practically trip over my feet. Nightly simply sweeps me into his arms. "I like the sound of that." He nuzzles into my neck.

I can't have heard him correctly. "What?!"

"We agreed we're keeping each other. We *kissed* on it," he reminds me.

This man, not afraid of a damn thing. "I guess we did."

"Good." He kisses my cheek, closing us into his room with a click of the lock. "Now, I'm going to need you naked."

CHAPTER 22

NIGHTLY

AS I TAKE IN EM'S BEAUTIFUL, STRONG, COMPLETE-ly-bare-to-me, body, I'm struck again by her resilience. She didn't hesitate when I voiced my need to have her naked. I wasn't joking, but I could have been more sensitive given the details she shared today.

I join her on the bed and apparently hesitate for a moment too long. She grips my wrist, firmly placing my hand on her breast. "Please don't treat me with kid gloves; don't make me feel like I'm broken." She firmly grips my chin. "And don't you dare pity me."

"Em..." Emotions clog my throat, stealing my voice. I bury my face in her shoulder, tugging her closer, holding her tighter than can be comfortable.

She wraps around me instead of pulling away. "It's okay, Carter. *I'm* okay." She kisses my neck, sending tingles down my back. "Please don't see me differently."

"It's not that," I rasp. "I'm in awe." I pull back, needing her golden eyes, fierce like a lion but, at the moment, tender like a teddy bear. "You honor me with your trust. I don't want to fuck it up. I want this, Em. What we have. I want it so fucking much. Please have grace for me when I fuck up, for I surely will—not just in bed but out. You shared your triggers, and I'll, of course, honor them. But if, in the heat of the moment, I say or do something stupid, please give me a chance to make it better."

"Carter…" Her teary reply rips up my chest, obliterating the emptiness that lived there before her.

"I care for you so much, Em. It scares me how much already. I don't want to scare you off by admitting it too early, yet I can't have you believing this is a casual thing for me. I'm talking about keeping you, and I mean it. We're talking forever here. You in my home or me in yours, the first face I see in the morning and the last each night. A home full of babies, and a dog or a cat—hell, both if you want. Vacations and holidays, making our own traditions. I want it all, beautiful. I want it all with you."

Tears stream down her face as she grips the back of my neck, smashing her mouth to mine. "This mouth." She grinds her heated flesh against mine, making me groan. "God…" she breathes across our kiss, effortlessly flipping our positions so she's on top, straddling my hips, moving her wet pussy along my cock.

"You make me ravenous." She rises up and impales herself on my cock, stealing my breath. No warm-up, no chance to ease her into it. She just takes what she wants. And I'm here for it.

I grip her hips, not to guide, but to steady myself, to focus on her and not the heat of her wet pussy swallowing me whole, over and over as she moves with grace and determination to fuck me senseless.

"Fuck, Em. Slow down. Make it last, baby." Sliding my hands along her silky body, strong and powerful as she undulates over me, I squeeze one breast and capture the back of her neck to bring her down for a kiss. "You keep fucking me like this, and I'm going to come too soon."

"Yes," she pants, placing her hand over mine over her breast. "Fill me up, Carter. Give it to me."

Jesus, this woman. I pinch her nipple and swallow her moan in a fiery kiss. I'm not coming before she does. I give up my hold on her neck and slide my hand between us. She cries out when I make contact with her clit, rubbing in steady circles. She falters for only a second, bracing on my shoulders, changing her angle, grinding deeper with every swipe of her clit. "Fuck, Em. So fucking wet. Can you hear it? The sounds of you fucking me?"

"Carter!" Her whole body shudders as she soaks my cock.

I grit my teeth to keep my release at bay. *Not fucking yet!* "Are you gonna come for me, beautiful?" The thought nearly does me in. I pinch her nipple, rise up enough to capture it with my mouth, and bite down hard enough to set her off, not hard enough to leave a mark.

She shatters, her pussy squeezing the ever-loving life out of my cock. I cry out around her breast then suck hard as I pound my release into her, and into her, and into her. Each pulse a reminder of how lucky I am to have her in my arms, in my life, and if I'm lucky, in my bed for the rest of our lives.

EMMELINE

"Oh my God!" I wiggle under his ministrations. His tongue is doing wicked, wicked things to the very place he just unloaded into. How? He doesn't seem to care as he fucks me with his tongue and sucks my clit like he did my nipples mere minutes ago, blowing my mind with an orgasm that stole my breath and my sight.

And now. Now, he's feasting between my legs like I'm the dinner he sacrificed to bring me to his bed to have sex. It's not just sex though. It's everything he said he wanted and more. He so easily voiced my every dream for my life as if he wasn't blowing up my world with the words coming out of his incredibly talented mouth.

There should be awards for how gifted he is with his sweet talk, his dirty talk, and the way his tongue reaches into me, seeking every ounce of my pleasure.

His fingers dive into me, drilling that place that has my legs shaking and wetness gushing. "Carter!" I arch off the bed. "I need your cock!" I need it like my next breath. I need it nearly as bad as I need to come, and I want to squeeze him when I do.

"You'll have it, beautiful. As soon as you come." He keeps promising, each time he takes me to the edge and backs off, only to take me there again and again.

"Then make me come!" I grip the back of his head, shoving my pussy into his face. I'm not sure how he's even breathing. Maybe he's so talented, he has gills that let him breathe through my juices.

His chuckle only spurs me on. "Working on it." His fingers slip lower, teasing the space between my holes. A gasp of pleasure has my abdominal muscles twitching and my hips tilting for more.

"Do it." I caress his cheek. His eyes meet mine, and the sight of his mouth moving over my clit has my head falling back. "Touch me there. Make me come, Carter." I give the permission I never thought I could.

Slowly, his fingers delve lower, slick and arousing, moving ever closer. I gasp at the first swipe and cry out as he pinches my nipple at the same time, doing it again and again. Rewiring my brain, one delicious touch at a time. He doesn't breach, only circling.

Then both hands are there, filling me and rubbing my clit and my asshole. So damn talented. He bends over me, catching my gaze. "You're so fucking hot, Em."

He presses his Em-soaked lips to mine, feeding me my essence as he finger-fucks my pussy, and then he does it. He presses into that dark recess I never wanted to experience again. Slowly he presses as I press back, wanting more… *needing* more.

In a move that steals my breath, he slips inside, just a finger that feels as big as his cock. "Carter," I gasp. "Oh my God."

His mouth is back on my clit, licking and sucking as he fills me completely. Stroke for stroke, I moan my consent, my elation. His touch and the sounds of what he's doing to my body mixed with his raw growls as he eats up my pleasure send me soaring. I fly so high, I fear I'll never fall over the edge.

And then I do. On a scream that rips up my throat, I explode. My orgasm detonates throughout my body in a shockwave as fluid gushes from between my legs.

"Fuck, baby. Just like that." He laps it up, somehow still working my clit as each wave echoes through my body and into the room in panting gasps and shuddered cries.

Tenderly, so damn tenderly, Carter comes over me, pressing kisses and heated touches to my body as he rests over me and slips his cock inside. Slow, delicious strokes send my limbs shaking with aftershocks. He whispers praise and adoration along my neck and face. Gentle kisses ease me back to him, awakening desire with new pleasure, with need to be filled and filled and filled in ways I never thought possible.

With him, I'm not broken. I'm not ruined by my past. I'm whole, not because he makes me so, but because he sees me as so. I am precious. I am seen. I am accepted. I dare say loved—by him.

He moves over me, in me, wrapped around me, cocooned.

Soul-to-soul, eye-to-eye, he makes love to me with tender strokes and loving touches, delving in deep and grinding, building and building, taking and giving. Filling my heart to near bursting until we come with teary gazes locked on one another, calling each other's names as I squeeze him and he fills me. And I. Am. Whole.

In his arms, I drift to sleep with dreams of a future with him dancing in my head.

CHAPTER 23

NIGHTLY

TONIGHT'S OUR FIRST AWAY GAME AND THE toughest opponent yet for the season. The big-headed New York Crushers won the cup last year. They're riding the high of a great season with sights on a repeat. We're here to show them it's not possible. We're taking this win on their home ice, in front of their fans, who are screaming and booing us like we're kicking puppies and raising taxes. The crowd is insane, and it only feeds our hunger, our determination to rule. They're good. I'll give them that. But we're better, hungrier, and well rested after having yesterday off.

I slept the entire flight here, needed the rest after the incredible night with Em—*my* girl. We promised. We kissed on it.

The thought of her feeds my determination to play well for my team, make them and her proud. She's watching on TV with Bennett and Willa on the massive screen in my theatre room. Wall-to-wall me and the team, making her proud. We didn't use the room yesterday to watch movies, mainly because we got comfortable on the couch after lunch, and no one wanted to move. I showed Bennett how the set-up works before I left this morning to catch the team bus to the airport.

Though, I wouldn't be surprised if they're chilling in the living room instead. The theatre room is pretty much a waste. It's never used. I should turn it into a game room or something kid-friendly for when the time comes. I don't know if I'll be with the Dragons by then, but I don't have any intention of leaving. It doesn't mean it won't happen.

The thought steals my concentration from the game as I take a breather on the bench. What if I get traded? Would Em do long-distance? Would she come with me? Would it be fair to even ask that of her? Shit. What about Bennett? What about Lotti's?

"Let's go!" Kells slaps my shoulder as he hops over the wall. On instinct, I follow, slapping sticks with Storm as I take his place in the changeover.

It's second period, and we're up 3-0. I don't want to just hold on to the lead. I want to demolish NY's hope of ever beating us, this season or next. We skate hard, working in concert with each other, taking advantage of their inflated egos and underestimating what a fine-tuned team we are.

I face off with their center, slap the puck to Alec, who passes to Kells, back to me, and I catch Alec as he skirts another defender. He spins around, passing it between his legs and circling back around like a dance to pass it again through their legs to grab it on the other side, spinning and circling with them trailing behind like a conga line heading to our o-zone. He fakes hitting to the right, only to backhand it between the goalie's legs and into their net. It's a beautiful goal. The few fans we have here go crazy.

We change over, resting for sixty seconds before switching again, same lines, different dance. Each time we take the puck to their end and score or get really damn close.

Third period, clock almost out of time, we've got a power play—NY is a man down due to a penalty. Alec gets me the puck, and I break away ahead of everyone else. It's just me and their goalie. His eyes are locked on me, the puck back and forth between my skates and stick.

Last second, I spin, skating backwards, taking in the players who rush toward me at breakneck speed. Then, as I twist back to the goalie, I catch the top right corner of the net with a one-handed wrist shot. Goal. Maybe not as pretty as Alec's dancing conga line, but it'll do.

We win 7-1. Not a shutout but pretty darn close.

EMMELINE

I scream—we scream—like idiots watching Nightly play. We're on our feet, on the edge of our seats, hooting and hollering at the TV like they can hear us, and when they score, we celebrate like we won the lottery. It's exhilarating, and Willa is right there with us, celebrating her brother with pride that only makes me like her more.

I got the impression Nightly's parents and brother aren't the most supportive or close to Nightly, but his sister is a whole other story. She talks about him with so much pride. I'm happy we got to meet. Moreover, I'm happy he has her in his corner. She doesn't seem to mind sharing that corner with Bennett and me either.

I'm exhausted by the time I crawl into Nightly's bed. He asked us to stay over, if we wanted. He liked the idea of me—us—in his space. He also wanted to be sure his sister had some company if she wanted it. She did sleep in the pool house. Bennett stayed in one of the many guest rooms in the main house with me. Though, I think if B had been willing, Willa would have gladly shared her bed with him.

Tomorrow is game two of three, and if they play like they did tonight, it'll be equally exciting and another win on their road to the Stanley Cup. I'm on the countdown till he comes home. Home? Back in town?

Though Lotti's was busy, the day slinked by in slow motion knowing I wouldn't see Nightly for three more days. Once home, he'll have a day of rest on Friday, then light practice before the home game on Saturday.

My phone chimes as I'm channel-surfing from his bed. I mute the TV as Nightly's name appears on my screen with a text.

> **CARTER/NIGHTLY:** *Hi, beautiful. Did I wake you?*

> **ME:** *Hi! No, I'm up. Congrats on the win. It was an awesome game!*

> **CARTER/NIGHTLY:** *I played better knowing you were watching. You're my lucky charm.*

A laugh bubbles out. He's insane but sweet.

> **ME:** *Crazy talk. It's your skill that made you play so well. The whole team was amazing.*

> **CARTER/NIGHTLY:** *Where are you?*

> **ME:** *Your bed. It's kinda lonely without you. I can smell you on the sheets.*

Embarrassingly, we had to change the sheets before finally going to sleep yesterday. Sex is messy business, especially with his skills making my body gush like a fire hydrant.

CARTER/NIGHTLY: *Damn, woman. Don't make me hard. I'm on a plane surrounded by guys.*

ME: *I think I could just look at you, and you'd get hard, based on last night.*

CARTER/NIGHTLY: *Yes, but the idea of you in my bed naked without me is cruel.*

ME: *Who said I'm naked?*

CARTER/NIGHTLY: *Don't ruin the fantasy.*

ME: *Would never. Go on… I'm naked…*

CARTER/NIGHTLY: *There you go again, making me hard.*

CARTER/NIGHTLY: *Damn, I have to go. We're getting ready to take off. I don't know how tomorrow will go, but I'll call when I can.*

ME: *Okay. Night.* 💋

CARTER/NIGHTLY: *G'night, baby.* ❤

I stare at his heart emoji entirely too long. It's embarrassing. It's also really sweet.

The next three days pass in a blur of working out in Nightly's gym each morning with Bennett, going to work, delivering fresh food to the shelter, and back to Nightly's for dinner and the Dragons game.

They won all three games. Bennett says this is their year. The team is primed to go all the way to cup finals. How exciting is that?

I didn't play sports growing up. It was just Mom and me. There wasn't time for much else other than school and work. I've worked nearly every day of my life since I was twelve. Even if I wasn't at a paying job, it was homework, cooking, cleaning, and trying to stay safe and out of trouble. I don't have any idea what it's like to succeed in a sport and be recognized by the association and peers for your success.

I've come close to relating, being a decorated Marine. Though it often wasn't celebrated beyond a plaque, a medal, or an additional insignia on my uniform. Any recognition, for the most part, wouldn't be widely known outside the Marines or those serving in political office. It's not like winning a championship in a sport you excel in, where it's televised, and fans come to cheer you on. The world of professional sports is a completely different creature. Not complaining. The last thing I want to be is famous. Well known, maybe, for being the best coffee shoppe in Colorado—or at least the Denver area. Even then, it would be Lotti's getting the recognition and not me, specifically.

Sometime in the night early Friday, Nightly climbs into bed, wrapping around me, warming me from the outside in—my body and heart. Whispering sweet nothings along my shoulder and neck, he showers me with tender kisses until I drift off to sleep. Confirming I am, in fact, home.

CHAPTER 24

NIGHTLY

WAKING UP TO EM IN MY BED FEELS LIKE ALL THE parts of my life locking into place. Oblivious to my happy-place moment, she insists she needs to leave the warmth of our bed to work out.

Holding her to me as she weakly tries to escape, I mumble into her neck, "I've helped create a monster."

She snickers and relaxes. "You'll benefit later from the extra energy working out affords me."

"Shh. Sleep, baby." Exhausted, I fall back asleep with her in my arms.

I come back to the waking world to the sound of the shower, an otherwise quiet house, and the space next to me cold and empty.

After so many days on the road, I'm sore and in need of coffee and perhaps more sleep. There's no mandatory practice today. Though, I might go in later for the light skate, help stretch my muscles, stay loose for tomorrow's game.

As I stretch, a ping from my phone has me slowly moving to the dresser to see if it's urgent or can wait until I'm fully conscious.

I groan as I read the group chat with Austin, my agent, and Angela, my PR person.

> **AUSTIN:** *Great job last night, Nightly! Don't forget the charity event tonight. Angela said she'd go with you if you changed your mind about a date.*

Damn, I didn't check my schedule for today other than knowing going to The Lair was optional. I was hoping to spend the day with Em. And take Angela to the gala? No. I don't mix business with perceived pleasure. She's an employee, and I'd never date her or want to give the impression that I am. I totally want to blow off the event. I won't. I've committed, and it's for a good cause.

> **ME:** *Thanks. Just woke up. Give me time to consider tonight. But if I go, I'll have my own date.*

> **AUSTIN:** *Okay, big guy. Let me know when you've had some coffee. And who?*

> **ME:** *My girl, Emmeline.*

My phone keeps pinging. I can only imagine all the questions he has for me about Em and my claiming her as mine when I'm ostensibly perpetually single. I silence my phone and turn it facedown. They can wait. First things first. I need Em, then coffee.

EMMELINE

Cool air hits my back when the shower door opens and closes. Nightly steps in, gloriously naked in all his muscled perfection.

It's not fair how gorgeous he is. Dark hair, blue eyes, tight jawline, perfectly formed pecs sitting atop ideal washboard abs, all held up by massive thighs that give him speed on the ice and undeniable strength to obliterate me with his not-to-be-overlooked sizeable cock.

I'd be self-conscious if the desire in his eyes didn't convey how much he likes what he sees when he looks at me. My skin prickles, and my nipples tighten in anticipation.

"You left me alone in bed." He steps into the stream of water, his whole body blanketing the back of mine, gripping my hips and nuzzling my neck.

"I had to work out first thing, or I wouldn't get it done." I lean into him, tilting my head, encouraging more of his sensuous shoulder and neck kisses.

"Hmm," rumbles along my spine. "I want to support healthy habits." He squeezes my breasts, teasing my nipples while rubbing his hard length against me.

"Carter," I gasp and grip his thighs, rocking into him.

"I need to be inside you," he growls along my heated skin. My muscles flex as he runs his hand down my ticklish and sensitive stomach, cupping my mound before probing fingers slip through my pussy lips. His entire hand moves, fingers sinking inside, his palm rubbing my clit with each motion. "Fuck, Em. I've missed you."

My heart thumps its approval. "Missed you too." I turn my head, palming the back of his neck to capture his mouth. He dives in, sucking, soothing, caressing, his tongue working me like his fingers. In and out, steady, slow pressure with tender force that has my legs trembling and my other arm gripping his, playing my breasts like a stress ball, paying extra attention to my nipples. They're needy like that.

"Please," I beg, inundated with pleasure swirling and building, the need for release almost too much.

"Fuck. You make me so damn hard. I'm gonna fill you full of cock as soon as you come, beautiful," he promises around our kiss, sucking my lower lip as he pinches my nipples, one then the other.

His dirty mouth throws me to the edge of oblivion, but it's his growl of approval that plummets me over the edge, crying out as I squeeze and come around his fingers. His embrace tightens, holding me up as I quake and shiver in his arms. "So fucking beautiful," he breathes into our kiss, fucking me through every tremor until I'm a panting mess, wet and wrung out.

"Hands against the wall," he rasps in my ear, guiding my hands on the cool tiles. "Spread, baby." He uses his foot to widen my stance and runs both hands through my soaked pussy, one from the front, the other from the back, spreading my juices, making me moan. "Gonna fuck you now, Em. Hold on."

He grips my hip and thrusts, filling me in one smooth motion.

"Oh, fuck!" I shout, fighting to hold my position as he pounds into me, deep and hard. "Yes!"

"Too fucking long, Em. I've missed the feel of you around my cock. Four days is too fucking long," he growls, nipping at my neck then sucking the sting away.

Arching, pressing back as he thrusts forward, I practically claw the wall, needing, needing, needing—every word, growl, moan, every thick inch of his perfect cock. His body drills into mine, marking me, taking and giving. I'm delirious, so turned on, picturing him taking me over every surface of his house, filling me so completely, his essence dripping out of me for days.

"Fuck. You keep squeezing me like that, I'm gonna come too soon."

"Then you can just do it again."

He drills harder, gripping my hip so tight it'll bruise, and runs his other hand around to rub my clit.

"Yes!" I cry. "So close!"

"You can't get enough of my cock, can you, Em?" Deeper, harder, he fucks me, latching onto my neck and biting. Hard.

"No. I need you all the time! Please, Carter. Make me come." Gah, who am I?

"Goddammitbaby!" His growl reverberates off the shower walls as he comes. One carefully placed slap over my clit shatters me, coming so hard I nearly fall. Shoved flat against the tiles, he pumps into me, showering my insides with his release, each shot sending another quake through my body.

"Fuck," he exhales, his forehead hitting my shoulder. "I've missed you."

My chuckle barely has any air behind it. "I can tell."

"Did I hurt you?" The worry in his voice has me turning, causing us both to groan as his semi hard cock slips free.

I kiss his face, capturing his eyes. "No, you didn't hurt me. It was—"

"Incredible," he completes, relaxing.

"Yeah. Pretty incredible." I seize his mouth, expressing my thanks and every bursting emotion into our kiss. What I feel for him is almost too much. He's become essential, and that scares me to death. But I'm no quitter. I'm here for it—for us.

He kisses me back, his hands roaming, kneading, arousing.

Before it gets too heated, he pulls back, grabs the soap and starts cleaning us up. Soon as his cock hardens and new arousal takes me, he lifts me by my thighs to wrap around him and thrusts back inside my well-loved pussy, claiming, "I don't want you to ever leave."

CHAPTER 25

NIGHTLY

AFTER OUR SHOWER, WE DRESS AND HEAD TO the kitchen, both in dire need of coffee. We find Bennett and Willa cooking breakfast, looking rather chummy. Em and I share a look. She shrugs and shakes her head yet beams at her bestie.

"Morning," Willa sing-songs, entirely too chipper, remining me of the old Willa that was always cheery, before life ran her over a time or two.

"G'morning." I give her a side-hug before pulling Em to the kitchen bar to sit.

"Morning, Puddin'. Sleep okay?" Bennett places a mug of coffee made exactly as she likes in front of her.

"I did, especially once Nightly got home." She presses a kiss to the back of my hand, holding it as she takes a tentative sip.

He turns to me. "Sugar and creamer, right?"

"Yes, please." I sit beside my girl.

"What time did you get in?" Willa asks, checking the bacon in the oven.

"Around 1:00 a.m." I thank Bennett for the cup of joe and

watch Willa and Bennett work side by side. It doesn't seem like this is the first morning they've cooked together. The thought doesn't bother me as it might have at one time. They're adults. Both had hard times, and if they find a little comfort in whatever it is they're doing, I'm not here to judge or be an obstacle to overcome. They've overcome enough.

My phone vibrates in my pocket. I pull it out and see more texts from Austin and Angela. I quickly scan the messages and set it aside. "Em, I've got a charity event tonight. I know it's last minute, but would you go with me?"

Em's mug pauses halfway to her mouth. "Tonight? What kind of event? How dressy are we talking?"

"It's a gala, so pretty dressy."

Her eyes only widen farther. "I don't—"

"I can have some dresses sent over for you to choose from. Or we can go shop—"

"She'll go." Bennett sets plates loaded with eggs, bacon, and toast in front of us. "Have dresses and shoes sent over." He bops Em on the nose. "This one hates to shop."

"But I've got work—" she begins.

"Nice try! I'll handle Lotti's," Bennett interjects. "You take the food to Joey, bring Nightly to help. Then come back here, have plenty of time to figure out which dress to wear and get all gorgeous for your night out."

Damn, he's got Em down pat. I hate to say he's handling her, but I'm pretty sure this is what handling looks like, at least for them. She was on the verge of panicking. He stepped in, eased her load, ensuring a clear path to what needs to be done. No fuss. No muss.

Only, "Who's Joey?"

"He's the executive director for Raven's Hope," Bennett advises.

"The charity you told me about, right?" I ask Em.

"Yeah. It would be a good opportunity to meet him and check the place out, if you want. But you probably have practice or—"

"No." I kiss her forehead. "No practice today, it's a recovery day. I'll check out your charity, and you can come to my charity event tonight."

She narrows her eyes. "Are you negotiating with me? Tit for tat?"

"Baby," I nuzzle her neck, "you're the one with the tits, and I don't have any tats."

She shoves me playfully. "You know what I mean."

I grip the back of her neck. "We don't have to do either. It just seems like a good opportunity to check out Raven's Hope and see what I can do to help out this Joey." I press a tender kiss to her mouth. "And I've already committed to the gala tonight. I can't in good conscience cancel, and I really don't want to go alone. I'd rather have you on my arm."

She points to my sister. "You could take Willa."

"Oh, no. I'm not going to some fancy-schmancy charity thing where everyone kisses my brother's ass. Thanks, but no thanks." She hands Bennett his plate. "Besides, Benny and I have plans."

"Benny?" Em teases. I've heard her call him that a time or two, and he always balks at it.

"Shut it, Puddin'." He scowls at her, then winks a second later.

"Okay, *Benny*. You have fun on your date, and I'll have fun on mine." Em nods, decision made.

Finally, a real date. I couldn't be happier about it. I squeeze my woman's hand, kissing her cheek. "Thank you."

"Welcome," she halfheartedly grumbles.

EMMELINE

Fresh out of the shower, I manage to get my hair and makeup done and slip on my *underthings*—Nightly's term for panties and bra is growing on me—before he traipses into the bathroom. I nearly swallow my tongue. He's a well-formulated, amped-up, darker *007* in his black tux with white shirt and black bow tie to *nearly* complete the ensemble. Over his impressive shoulder span, I spot his jacket draped over the edge of the bed.

"Damn, Night." I saunter over, wanting to devour every glorious inch of my delicious man.

He snags me around the waist, pulling me in, nipping at my bottom lip as I wrap my arms around his shoulders, pleased to find myself eye level with his chin in my stilettos I'm sure to regret by the end of the night. "I'm not sure it's fair to the rest of mankind letting you out in public looking this hot."

"Em," he growls, his large, callused hands traversing my near nakedness.

I bat my heavy lashes, trying to hide the effect he's having on me. "I mean, have some pity on the rest of the poor, average, non-deity men in the world who will never know an ounce of the sexiness you exude just by breathing."

"Fuck, baby. Your mouth and this fucking body." His mouth lands on my neck as he squeezes my ass, separating my cheeks and delving in.

"Oh, fuck," I moan, completely unprepared for the fingers he slips inside me, fucking me in deep, probing strokes. "Carter, we—"

"No, Em. I've had to keep my hands off you all day—"

"Not in the shower." I hold on as he kicks my foot out to widen my stance, running his tongue along the seam of my mouth. *Thank God for lip stain.*

"That was this morning." He lifts me with one arm around my waist, fingers fully planted in my core, stopping when my legs hit the counter. He removes his fingers, devilishly slowly, and sets me down on the cool stone, shocking the air out of my lungs.

"I'm talking about watching you work your magic at Raven's Hope," he removes my thong swiftly, discarding it over his shoulder, "delivering food," he pops the clasp on my bra and dumps it nearly in the same puddle as my panties, "you made and clothes," he shoves his fingers back inside me, "you collected—"

"Lotti's collected—" I barely manage to interject before he starts pumping his fingers, rubbing my clit, and sucks a nipple deep. "Jesus, Carter." I can't even think straight. *How's a man so friggin hot this hot for me?*

He growls in my face, "Don't ever say that again, much less think it."

"What—" I didn't realize I voiced my deepest fear—he's too good for me. Too handsome. Too nice. Too sexy. Too rich. Too famous. Too undamaged. "I'm just me," I plead, needing him to understand. In seconds, his hands are gone from my body. "No!"

"I have to show you." His pants and boxer briefs fall to his feet, his tie is discarded, and his shirt is undone, leaving his chest and rippled abdomen bare. Gripping his cock, he settles between my spread legs.

Words fail me as I succumb to the spell of his well-formed obliques and the draw of each rough stroke of his imposing length.

"Em?"

The gravel in his voice has me ripping my eyes away from his hand to his face. "Yeah?"

"I need you to hear me." He angles his tip, pushing forward, then lifts my leg with a hand under my knee, bringing it to the crook of his arm, and thrusts inside.

"Oh, God." I grip the counter and his shoulder, trying not to tip over or bash into the mirror. "How do you expect me to listen with your cock inside me?"

The corner of his mouth tips. "Try, baby. Try really fucking hard." He punctuates his last word by pulling out and slamming into me over and over.

I cry out each and every time.

"This *friggin' hot man* is so fucking in love with you, everything about you turns me on and makes me *hot*. Do you understand? *You* do this to me," thrust, "only you," three deep and hard thrust, thrust, thrust, "get me this worked up, this fucking hard. I lose my goddamned mind over you."

"Carter!" I wrap around him, hugging him, holding on as he fucks me into the counter.

"I fucking love you, do you hear me?!"

"Yes!" I come so hard, I choke on a sob. He hit something loose, knocked it free, and now I can't stop crying.

I'm a sobbing mess as he discards the rest of his clothes, picks me up, walks to his bed and lays me down. He falls over me, filling me so completely, I cry even harder. Pumping slowly, kissing me tenderly, he grinds and strokes me inside and out. "I love you, Emmeline Weston. Please don't fucking doubt that or my attraction to you, my want of you."

"Carter," I capture his face, rubbing my thumbs along his jaw and chin, "what are you doing to me?"

"Loving you, Em. This is what love looks like—at least, my love," he chokes out and buries his head in my neck.

"Our love," I correct.

"What?" He lifts his head, meeting my gaze. "Say that again?"

"This is what *our* love looks like." I press a kiss to the mouth I love so much, it hurts. "I love you, Carter. I'm scared as shit about it. But I love you. I'm done fighting it, trying to talk myself out of it. I want to be loved by you, but mostly," I close my eyes and then open them again, "I want to love you the way you deserve—with everything I have."

"No take-backs." He kisses along my neck to my ear, pressing his smile into mine as our lips meet.

"No take-backs."

"Good." He rears back, gripping my legs. "Now, I need you to come again." He thrusts as his thumb rubs my clit. "Need you to soak my cock, our sheets. I want to remember the feel of you squeezing me so damn good I can't wait to get home tonight to do it again."

"What? We're still going?"

He looks at me like I'm crazy. "Yep."

"But I'm a mess. I've been crying—"

"You're a beautiful mess, and you'll clean up just fine." He pinches my nipple, picking up the pace. "No more talking, Em. Only screaming my name."

"Carter!" I cry when he slaps my clit.

"Yep, just like that, but louder." He does it again and again.

By the time he fills me with his release, I've orgasmed two more times, I'm hoarse from screaming his name and many other unintelligible words, and I did soak his sheets—our sheets—and his—my—cock. He screamed my name too. I felt it deep in my soul, right along with the place his love now lives. Safe and secure.

CHAPTER 26

EMMELINE

I WANT TO SLAP THE SMUG SMILE OFF NIGHTLY'S face. But that'll never happen. One, I don't believe in violence, except in extreme cases where it's required to subdue a bad guy or protect those you love. And two, the handsome man next to me loves me and I love him. Three—and more to the point—I'm not really irritated. I'm embarrassed and out of my league. He's so smooth and comfortable in his skin and elevated role as an elite pro athlete. I'm the bumbling buffoon at his side so sex drunk I gave the reporter my name—my full name… not just Lotti's Latte.

Maybe somewhere in the back of my skull I thought it would bring Lotti's more business, not that we need it. We're barely holding on with how busy we are. Some days, I need double the staff and space to serve all the customers who come through our doors or order online for pickup or delivery. I don't know how we manage it most days, and on others, I'm fairly certain we don't. We fulfilled orders, but did we do it with a smile or more likely a rushed, *Thank you, come again!* before moving on?

I sigh deeply once we get across the red carpet and into the venue. Nightly did give me a heads-up and offered to let me go around and meet him inside. But I'd just exclaimed my love for the man. Told him I wanted to love him the way he deserves—and this man deserves to be loved in public. Not a secret I keep to myself or only our small, safe world where we don't let anyone else in. He doesn't deserve that kind of selfish love. He needs love that lives out loud, in broad daylight, in front of the media—if only a time or two until it's known he has someone. He's mine, and I'm his.

"Thanks for walking the gauntlet with me." He kisses the curve of my neck, sending shivers down my back as we make our way to the bar. "I've never walked into a venue with someone who's *really* with me, not a staged date for publicity's sake."

The warmth and gratitude in his gaze have my shoulders relaxing and fortifying myself for the next round of social challenges. "You're welcome." I'd like to say I was happy to do it, but *happy* would be a stretch.

"What do you want to drink?" He orders a near beer, not wanting to drink with a game tomorrow.

"Just ice water, please." I don't need alcohol, which would perhaps lessen my nerves but would also dull my senses. I've already proven I can't be trusted not to give out details a reporter has no business knowing, least of all from my own lips.

Drinks in hand, Nightly motions to a group of guys standing near a table. "Let's say *hi* to the guys before making the required rounds."

Introductions made, I find myself surrounded by men, impressive in size and looks, who are far more reserved and well-mannered than anticipated. Davi and Tate, the Dragons' goalies, rib on each other. The same for Nightly and Storm, both centers. Then there are Alec and Kells, left and right wings, who practically finish each other's sentences. They're a tight-knit group.

"So, Emmeline. You should come hang with us after a game."

Tate bumps Nightly's shoulder. "Give us a chance to get to know our captain's girl." *See if I'm worthy,* I hear.

"*Or* you could come over and *hang* and get to know me in a less puck bunny-filled, alcohol-laced environment," falls from my lips before I can censor myself.

Nightly pulls me into his side and kisses the top of my head. "You tell 'em, baby."

"I'm sor—" I start, but Tate waves me off, not a bit put out. "Bars aren't really my scene," I say instead. They're one of my least favorite places—too crowded, too loud, and sometimes unpredictable.

Storm smiles, tapping his beer to my glass. "Don't apologize. You're right. We should get together on Sunday, grill steaks or burgers or whatever."

"You offering up your place?" Davi directs to Storm, but offers me a soft smile like he appreciates I don't need to be *seen* out in public with Nightly.

"Not my place." Nightly squeezes my hip. "We've got company, and I don't want to have to kick y'all out when you've overstayed your welcome."

"Fair." Tate seems to warm up a little. "I'll host. But you assholes have to bring food. I'm not feeding you cavernous motherfuckers."

Alec laughs. "Also fair."

"I could bring dessert," considering their size, I amend, "... or a couple of desserts." I catch Nightly's eyes. He's all smiles. I'm reminded how comfortable he is in his skin and with his friends—teammates. It's enviable.

"My sister and Em's best friend, Bennett, will probably come too," Nightly joins the conversation.

"Willa's in town?" Tate wags his brows.

"Don't even think about it," Nightly growls.

The guys laugh and continue planning and ribbing each other

like the friends they apparently are. It's nice to see. Reminds me of Bennett and me.

I only get a moment to consider what he and Willa are up to. In the rush to get out of the house and to Lotti's and then Raven's Hope, we didn't get any time to discuss what they had planned. In the next breath, my phone is vibrating. I ignore it with plans to check in a few when I excuse myself to go to the bathroom. But it starts up again.

Then Nightly's phone goes off.

Then a few of the other guys' phones.

Now, my heart is racing. It can't be a coincidence that all of our phones are going off. But why would mine be going off in sequence with theirs?

NIGHTLY

Em pulls her phone from her little black purse that matches her stunning dress. I'm in the process of digging mine out of my jacket pocket when it goes off again with text messages, then a phone call. The guys around me are doing the same.

"B—" Em answers and freezes. "What?!" Her eyes widen in shock.

"Em?" I move toward her, but she holds up her hand, stilling me.

"Um, Nightly?" Tate says from behind me.

"What do you mean it's gone viral? How is that possible? We haven't been here an hour." The color drains from her face.

A strong hand grips my arm. I turn just in time for Tate to shove his phone in my face. "We're all getting alerts."

I can't concentrate on the words swirling on the screen when all I see is Em practically running from the room, white as a ghost. It's got to be Bennett. I move to go after her, but Stone steps in front of me. "You need to see this—"

"No," I shove past him. "I need to get to my girl." I fly through the closest double doors that spill into the foyer and spot her slipping through a side door marked EXIT. I don't hesitate. Everything in me is screaming to get to Em, to protect her, to comfort her, do whatever the hell I need to do to make whatever is happening go away.

CHAPTER 27

NIGHTLY

I'M OUT OF MY MIND BY THE TIME I ARRIVE AT EM'S. She's not picking up, and neither is Bennett. On the way over, I talked to Angela, my PR person, who is reaching out to Charlie, the Dragons' head of PR, and Austin, my agent. Between the three of them, Summer with social media relations, and my lawyers, I'm hopeful they can nip this story in the bud.

My stomach rolls as visions of her bruised and swollen face in that news article from years ago echo in my mind. The visible damage those assholes did to her has me so on edge, I could seriously maim the next person who looks at her sideways. That is, if she gives me the chance to be anywhere near her. She's not answering my calls or texts, nor is she reaching out to discuss this. I know she's used to dealing with things on her own, but I thought we were a team.

I'm tempted to knock and immediately open her door. Instead, I knock and wait. I grip the doorframe when it's Willa who answers. "What the hell, Will? Why aren't any of you answering my calls?" I don't even try to hide my hurt.

"I'm sorry." She steps outside and closes the door behind her like she's not going to let me inside. "Bennett's trying to soothe Emmeline, but she won't stop crying," Willa's voice cracks. "I've haven't seen anyone so devastated, not since—" Tears stream down her cheeks.

I wrap her in my arms. "It's okay." I rub her back. "What's happening here has nothing to do with—"

"Don't say it," she pleads.

"Okay." All of this is setting off Willa's past as well. It's a complete clusterfuck of invasive reporting and victim shaming. "But you need to let me in so I can help."

She only nods and steps aside, letting me open the door. The second I enter, I hear my girl, and it's heart-wrenching. The sound—the vision—of any woman crying is difficult. But to hear my woman's misery is devastating. Layer on the fact I'm not the one comforting her, the whole thing has me mindless.

I rush to her bedroom. The door is ajar, the room glowing with soft light from a corner lamp and the wails of my girl filling the space surrounding her bed. She's wrapped in Bennett's arms, on his lap, where he's leaning against the headboard. She's fully dressed except her shoes which sit askew on the floor next to the bed. Em has her face buried in his neck, gripping him tightly, her whole body shaking with each wretched sob.

Bennett's eyes lift to mine as I approach. The brokenness I find there gives me pause. Is he having flashbacks too, or is he feeling her hurt? "Em." He gently rubs her shoulder, trying to get her attention. "Carter is here."

There's no response, no recognition, no deviation in her sobs except to catch the occasional breath.

I hesitate, wanting to sit, but I don't want to impose on their space even though everything in me demands I pull her into my arms and hold her until she's calm and knows she's safe with me.

He runs his fingers through her hair. "Em, Nightly is here."

Nothing.

He shakes his head. "She hasn't said a word since arriving home." A tear skates down his cheek. "She's never been like this—I've never *seen* her this distraught."

My resolve breaks. I can't stand apart from them any longer. I drop my jacket, loosen my tie and kick off my shoes, then climb on the other side of the bed, lying on my side, and reach for them. With his help, I manage to drag both into my arms with her between us.

Once she's solidly against my chest, he works his way lower till we're all three lined up, surrounding her with our love. I wrap my arm around her and him, and he does the same, squeezing, locking her between us. Tight, not enough to inhibit her air, but secure enough to induce a sensory deprivation-like calm. Hopefully.

"I'm here, Em. Please know I'll take care of this. I'm so sorry. I have my team working on it. I'm so sorry, baby." I kiss the back of her head. A modicum of relief washes over me as her shaking lessens and her sobs reduce to whimpers. "We're here. Bennett and I have you. You're safe. No one can hurt you."

Within a few minutes, she passes out from exhaustion. Slowly, I release Bennett, and he does the same, stretching out his arm. "How did you know that would work?" He eases up on his elbow to look down on us.

"I didn't. I was going on instinct. She needed something to snap her out of her spiral. I'd hoped feeling secure between us would work. Thankfully, it did." I catch his teary gaze. "You okay?"

He swipes at his face. "Yeah." He waves me off. "I don't know what I would've done if you hadn't shown up."

I hand him a tissue from the nightstand. "She would have fallen asleep eventually." I hope that would've been the case.

Thankfully, squeezing her between us worked. "Are you okay to stay with her for a bit longer? I really need to check in and see what's happening. I want as much resolved as possible before she wakes up."

"Yeah, just let me go to the bathroom and maybe change out of my jeans."

"Yeah, sure. Do whatever you need. I'll get her out of her dress and into something more comfortable to sleep in."

"I'll grab her something to wear." He eases away from her before getting up. "Just a sec." He disappears into her closet.

I've managed to unzip her dress by the time he returns with an oversized t-shirt. "She likes to sleep in this when she's having a hard day. She finds it comforting." He hands over the thinning shirt that is super soft. "I don't know why."

I don't care why. I only hope she forgives me for undressing her when she's not conscious. But there's no way sleeping in her curve-hugging dress can be comfy. I wait for him to close the door behind him, heading to the guest bedroom down the hall, before I work on removing her dress.

Once it's off, I unclasp her bra and carefully pull it free. Getting the t-shirt on over her head is fairly easy, and I manage to work it down her body without waking her up. She's dead to the world. I wish this reprieve would last a few weeks, give the world time to forget about the trending social media posts on nearly every platform. I'm nauseated at the idea of her waking up to that reality.

I get her under the covers and join her with the intention of leaving once Bennett returns. My last cognizant thoughts are a fantasy of getting on live TV to call out these cruel reporters and social media whores who thrive on the backs of another's misery and feel entitled to my woman's pain.

I'm roused awake, finding Bennett looming over me. "Sorry to wake you, but thought you'd rather make those important phone calls now than wait until the morning."

"Yeah. It's okay." I close my eyes for a second. "God, I just want to stay here and sleep with her, pretend none of this happened."

"You can—"

"No, you're right. I need to deal with this now, give them time to work their magic by morning." Hopefully. Or at least have a semblance of a gameplan to implement so we can hit the ground running. I scrub my face as I sit up. "You okay to sit with her?"

"Of course." He eases back in to the spot he vacated. "Willa made sandwiches if you want to grab something. You need to keep your fighting strength up. Plus, you have a game tomorrow."

I glance at the clock, thankful it's not yet tomorrow. I need to come back to bed as soon as possible. I'd skip the game if I didn't think it'd jeopardize the team. They don't deserve to suffer for this. As it is, I'll have a hard time concentrating. I won't let the media think they've hit a soft spot. If I do, it'll never end. Hurting the team hurts the fans, which hurts the franchise—and they don't deserve it either.

"Do you need anything?" I ask before leaving.

"No, just wake me up when you're ready to come back. I don't want to leave Willa alone out there."

"Sure. I appreciate you looking out for her."

"Hey, Nightly?"

With the door half open, I turn to meet his gaze.

"Make' em pay for hurting one of our own."

For a moment, I see the formidable warrior he is, the side he's hidden away out of necessity. But this battle may need a little of that warrior side to survive the media frenzy and fallout.

"Count on it." I pause again and add, "Thank you for always having her back. Know you both have me too."

A clenched jaw and a nod are all the response I get, but the gratitude in his eyes solidifies my resolve to keep him in our lives just as Em needs him to be. It's not my place to bulldoze her life because I love her and am here now. He was here first, and if their relationship changes, grows, that's between the two of them. My place is to love and support her wherever she is in life.

As soon as I shut her door, I call Austin to get an update and ensure he's gotten my lawyers involved. "Tell me where we are."

CHAPTER 28

EMMELINE

THE MORNING LIGHT COMING THROUGH THE curtains has me squinting and squeezing my eyes closed. They burn and begin to water. My head throbs, and my throat is parched. I feel hungover. I suppose an emotional hangover can be as disruptive as an alcohol-induced one.

I open my eyes to the sight of an empty bed. My heart aches at the idea I may have imagined Nightly coming in after me. Yet, I have a vague recollection of Bennett saying his name and the impression of Nightly holding me all night.

I don't *feel* like I was abandoned.

Slowly, I untangle my limbs from the covers. Noting my attire, a smile breaks free, lifting the dread weighing me down. I'm in my favorite oversized t-shirt. It was a gift from Mom, years ago. It's still my favorite comfy. I feel cared for even though I have no recollection how I got into it.

In the bathroom, I stop short when I catch my reflection in the mirror, flinching at my tear-stained, makeup-streaked face. I look hungover, worn out, strung out. Only one of those is true—I'm exhausted. Everything in me wants to climb back into bed and sleep for a week, maybe a month until the whole debacle blows over.

And it's sure to be a debacle.

Lotti's. I can't stomach the idea of facing the pitying looks, the pointed questions, the quiet murmurs. What advice would I give someone in my shoes, coming to me for guidance? It wouldn't be *stay in bed and pretend it never happened,* unfortunately.

I shower and scrub all evidence of yesterday off my face and body. It isn't enough. There's no protection from the haunting memories that come crashing in of the night so many years ago. Their touch—greedy and painful—the police, the hospital, the exam, the rape kit, my *mom* knowing what happened, having to witness it all on my face and my bruised body as I recovered. It wrecked her. I felt horrible for causing her worry and even a moment of displeasure. All of it echoes on repeat until I slam my palm against the shower tile and scream, "No!"

"Em?"

Nightly's raw voice penetrates my stupid, fumbling brain, and I freeze, mumbling, "I'll be out in a minute." I can't bring myself to look at him through the glass.

"I warmed your towels. Hurry, or they'll cool off."

I turn the shower off and run my hands over my hair, removing as much water as possible, then open the door. The cool air has me shivering. He hands me a towel. I use it on my hair, savoring the warmth on my face a second before flipping my head over and wrapping my hair in it. When I stand, he passes me another towel. I dry off as best I can and wrap it around my body, wishing it was even warmer and big enough to disappear in.

I step out. He backs up to give me room, then holds open my robe. I nearly collapse in tears at his thoughtfulness as he helps me slip on its cottony warmth. "Carter." He warmed my robe too.

"Shh, let me take care of you." He secures the tie around my waist, then tucks in the lapel up to my neck to ensure the warmth makes as much contact with my skin as possible. He carefully holds me to him, wrapping his arms around me.

I let out a deep sigh once, twice, and on the third time, I return his embrace, sinking into his chest, relishing the steady beat of his heart. He feels like home. The home I always wanted but never dreamed it would be with a pro athlete whose life—in turn, my life—is fodder for the masses.

I allow myself a few more moments of indulgence before reluctantly separating from him. "I don't think I can do this." My voice is a mere semblance of the certainty it usually holds.

"This?" He tips my chin to hold my gaze. "You don't have to do anything. Go back to bed and sleep. I'm sure you need it. Let me take care of everything. You need to eat something first, though." He moves for the door. "I'll be right back."

This man. He cracked my heart and my life wide open. Tears fall freely without permission. I use the sleeves of my robe to mop them up, but they keep coming at a freefall just like my life.

"I can't do you and me," my voice quivers, and I clear my throat as he stops and turns. "I can't do *this*," I restate with more authority.

"Em, please don't give up on us. It's a bump in the road. My team is working on silencing the story. The posts have been removed—"

"Nothing dies on the internet. It'll come up again, probably every time we're spotted by the media. You live in the spotlight. I live at Lotti's and in the background. I relish the quiet. Your life is anything but. I'm leery of men and crowds. You're surrounded by both. We're oil and water—"

He steps into me. "We're peanut butter and jelly. We fit. The perfect marrying of texture and flavor."

"Maybe I'm allergic—"

"You're not." He cups my cheek. "You love peanut butter, and you love me. I love you." He presses a tender kiss to my cheek. "I'm not my persona or my job. I love the quiet too. I love movies, naps, and cuddling with you—and Bennett—on the couch. I don't go to bars. I rarely drink. I'm only social for my job when it requires it of me, or for a good cause, like charities—like Raven's Hope."

"You're playing dirty." Bringing up what means so much to me.

"And you're choosing to focus on the bad side of fame. You're scared, and that's okay. We can work through that—together. Remember, you wanted my fame to bring awareness to Raven's Hope. You can't pick and choose what you like about my life. I'm a package deal too. I don't begrudge you your unique relationship with Bennett or judge how your trauma affects you. I want all of you. I *accept* all of you, which includes Bennett and your past."

"I can't confront my past every time I step outside. It'll be maddening. I don't want to be the girl who survived rape. It's not the totality of who I am." I scream the last part and stumble back till I hit the counter.

He follows, gripping my waist and the back of my neck. "No. It's not who you are, but it's a part of your story. You not only survived. You turned that tragedy into fuel. You learned to protect yourself. You joined the Marines. You served your country and furthered your skills. You use your tender heart that knows what it's like to be downtrodden and taken advantage of and protect your customers. You go above and beyond for a charity you have no connection to. You are amazing, and the world should know that side of you—who you are now. You only need to step out of the shadows and show them the badass you are."

I shrink back, slipping out of his hold and into my bedroom. "I can't." I don't have to defend my choices to him.

He follows, punching out a breath of air. "You mean you *won't.*

There's nothing you can't do, Em. I've seen it. I've *witnessed* it." He grips the back of my neck and kisses me, frustration rippling off him in waves. "I love you, Emmeline Weston, and I'm not giving up on us." And another kiss that steals my resolve. "I have to go to practice, then my game tonight. I can't flake on the team, as much as I want to stay here and fight with you."

I laugh through my tears. "You still want to fight with me?"

The fire in his eyes has me rethinking my entire stance. He swipes at my tears, bringing his forehead to mine. "It will be my privilege to fight with you for the rest of my days, Em."

With one last tender press of his lips to mine, he leaves, shutting my door behind him, leaving me stunned and uncertain in the middle of my room. This used to be my sanctuary. Now, it's cold and empty without him in it.

CHAPTER 29

NIGHTLY

IT TAKES EVERYTHING IN ME TO LEAVE, SHUTTING the door, leaving her alone with her demons.

Bennett trails me to the front door. "She scared you off then?"

I turn, wiping at my face and eyes. "Not even a little." I catch Willa's gaze over his shoulder. "She needs time. She's not ready to listen to reason or fight. Understandably. If I didn't have practice, a game, and a franchise depending on me, I'd stay and fight it out with her." I shake my head and meet his eyes. "She needs to want it. I can't make her want me more than she doesn't want to be in the public eye."

"Wait. So, what happens next?" He grips my arm before I grab the doorknob.

"Be here for her. Make sure she eats and sleeps. I'd avoid Lotti's for a few days. I'll continue to work on things on my end, and we'll see where we end up."

"You're not coming back?" Willa comes to stand beside Bennett, taking his hand. He smiles down at her, relief washing over him. I'm happy for them, but the sight of it hurts, knowing it should be me similarly bringing Em comfort—relief—but I can't.

"I don't know. She needs to come to the same conclusion I have. She has to want to fight for me—for us—for herself. But right now, all she sees is the devastation from the attack being thrown in her face. She's not feeling strong enough to confront it. Again, I understand. It just happened. It hasn't even been twenty-four hours. She needs time. I'm giving it to her."

"Did she ask for time?" Bennett stops me again.

"She said she couldn't do her and me, can't deal with everyone knowing she's a survivor." Am I betraying her by telling him this? I'm sure she'll tell him the same thing. Still, guilt rings through me.

"Damn." Bennett grips his hair. "She doesn't mean it."

"She does." I sigh. "Right now, she does."

I kiss Willa's cheek and grip Bennett's shoulder. "I have to go. I'm not giving up, but I can't hide out and pretend it didn't happen or convince her not to run away. I have to make it right as best I can without her by my side." With that, I slip out the door before they can stop me again. I sound like I have it all together, when really my heart is breaking. But I refuse to feel it, to dwell on it, to give in to the heartache.

I have commitments and a woman to fight for.

I'm not giving up on us.

EMMELINE

A knock at my door has me peeking out of my closet as I pull a shirt over my head. "Come in." I disappear inside for socks. I'm cold and need the extra layers.

"Hey." Bennett's sheepish gaze meets mine. "There's food."

"I could eat." I follow him out, ignoring my unmade bed, where Nightly's scent is sure to linger. I'm disappointed when I don't find him sitting on the couch with Willa. "Hey," I greet her. "I'm sorry about last night." I turn to Bennett. "You guys don't have to stay. I know you both have better things to do than babysit me."

"I do need to run to Lotti's. Show my face. Be sure things are running smoothly." He's done a great job of hiring employees who work great when we're there or not. But we're usually there.

"Then go. I'm going to hang here for a few days. Hope this thing blows over."

"You have vacation time you've never used."

I laugh. "So do you."

"Maybe we need to get better at taking time off." He glances at Willa. "I can drop you off on my way, or you could come with me."

She eyes ping-pong between the two of us. "If it's all the same to Em, I think I'll stick around. I wouldn't mind some downtime." She points to the TV." I was getting ready to watch a movie." Her gaze lands on B's. Their silent communication has me slipping into the kitchen in search of the food.

"Oven," Bennett hollers.

"Thanks." I groan in joy when I see all my favorite breakfast items he makes in covered dishes. "Did y'all eat?"

They come in, and B kisses my head. "I'll just make a biscuit to go."

"We were waiting…" Willa trails off, looking away.

I figure she was going to say they were waiting for Nightly and me. "Did he eat something before he…" I can't bring myself to say *left—before he left*. Before I *drove* him away?

Even though I know he did, his absence is palpable. He's a busy man who has more important things to do that sit with me while I wallow in my misery and push him away. I hold up my hand before they can respond. I don't want to know. It *hurts* to know. It hurts to think I may have pushed him away permanently.

I don't know how to traverse the gap between being with him *and* being with him in the public under the scrutiny of everyone knowing I was raped. Not just by one man, but two, in probably more detail than I would ever share with anyone besides the prosecutor and the police. Whether or not the news articles are accurate, it's out there in the world being replayed and rehashed over and over again on the internet—*and it's none of their business.*

Bennett makes a couple of breakfast biscuits before he goes home to shower and head to Lotti's. Willa and I fill our plates and get cozy on the couch with pillows and blankets, settling in for a day of movies and distracting entertainment.

After I finish my plate, I take hers and mine to the kitchen, leaving them in the sink to soak. Not because they need it, but because I don't feel like doing a productive thing today. Sadness sits heavy on my chest. Not over people knowing my secret, but over the way things ended with Nightly. I told him I couldn't do *this*—I couldn't do him and me.

Because I care more about what the world thinks of me than I care for him.

I'm a piece of shit.

I plop back down on the couch, catching Willa's eyes. "I think I screwed up."

She pauses the movie, waiting.

"I could feel like shit on my own *and* have a broken heart. Or I can feel like shit and still be with him." My chin trembles as my emotions rise up to kick my ass. "God, I'm an idiot."

She laughs, shaking her head. "You're human. You got scared. His celebrity is not nothing. But I've never seen him this happy and content. He was not happy to leave this morning, and even if you think you broke up with him—he has no intention of giving up on you. And he's still trying to fix this for you. A celeb trying to quell free publicity like this says something."

I stand and pace the length of the room and back. "We still have tickets for tonight's game, right?"

"Yes!" She stands, her smile spreading as she pulls out her phone. "I have an idea."

"What are you doing?" I'm a little afraid of her right now.

"I have a friend who's a producer at the *Today Show*."

"What?! That's national news—"

"You haven't seen how the story blew up overnight. It got picked up. It's no longer just local news, Em. Carter tried to stop it, but your story got a life of its own. Only, if you stand up—with Carter or without him—and tell your side of the story, you control the narrative. Put the bullies in their place. Take back your control. Show them it's not okay to use your trauma to make a buck."

"But won't I be doing the same, using my story to make the news?"

"You'll be using your story to shed light on survivors. Take back your power, Em. Let your voice outshine the ones spreading gossip."

"I just want to get Nightly back."

"That's easy," she brushes me off. "You show up at tonight's game, claim him as yours. Easy peasy—all's forgiven. But if you don't take this story by the horns and control the narrative, it's going to run you over. Get on the bull, Em, and show it who's boss."

Show it who's boss.

I call Bennett about going to the game as Willa calls her producer friend. I guess I'm riding this bull.

CHAPTER 30

NIGHTLY

ON MY WAY TO PRACTICE, I GET A CALL FROM Angela, who conferences in Austin, my agent. The story of Em and me has gone national. Because of her underage status when the assault happened, they did manage to get the original posts and article taken down, but it was too late to stop the flood of shares and screenshots that proceeded to rock the internet.

Colorado Dragons Center Carter McNight Dates Rape Victim

I want to puke. If I wasn't driving, I'd punch something or someone. I've never been ashamed of my semi-celebrity status until now. I'm a nobody, yet some asshole thought mine and Em's story was worth digging into. He couldn't just accept I was with a beautiful woman who owned her own business. He dug and dug until he struck blood to take her down—it certainly wasn't to build either of us up.

"I want to sue him," I bark at Angela.

"You can't sue for reporting the truth," Austin chimes in.

"Can't I?!" I blow out a tight breath. "What can we do?"

"We can ride it out—" Angela starts.

"I hate that idea. I need to defend her, make them see how wrong all of this is. It's her private life they're exposing to get headlines."

"Or we get in front of the story."

"How?" I'm hardly listening. All I want to do is get off the phone, turn around, and get back to my woman before she hears the news. "I've ruined her life."

"The animals who raped her did that," Austin reminds me.

"They didn't ruin her life." She's resilient. She persevered, made herself stronger. But, "The story never would've resurfaced if it wasn't for me," I remind them. "She never would have caught the public's eye unless Lotti's Latte went viral or something, and even then, maybe not." We'll never know, as that's not how it played out.

"It's out now, Nightly. We can't pull it back. We can't make it go away. All we can do is meet it where it is and tell your—*her* side. Bring it back to humanity, remind people there's a face behind the headlines," Angela offers, the level-headed one.

I grumble through the line, "I hate this."

"I know, man." Austin pauses. "Put this aside. Go to practice. We'll brainstorm, talk to your lawyers and the Dragons, and regroup later. Focus on your game as best you can. The best revenge is winning. Don't let this derail you."

"And Em?" I ask. "What the fuck is she supposed to do?"

"Stay home, don't talk to anyone," Angela reinforces what she texted me earlier, as though that's a solution.

After we hang up, I call Bennett. He answers on the first ring. "What the fuck, Nightly? I thought your people were going to handle this."

"So did I. How is she?"

"You know how she is. At least she's not crying in a fetal position like she was last night." He confirms what I hoped. Despite her saying she couldn't be with me under public scrutiny, she was still doing better than she was when I found her in Bennett's arms last night.

"Fuck, fuck, fuck," he barks. "Lock the door!"

"What's going on?" I nearly hit the curb turning into the underground employee parking garage at The Lair.

"The media just descended on Lotti's en masse. I'm going to have to shut down. I can't subject our customers or employees to this shit."

"I'm sorry, Bennett. I'll compensate you for the lost income. Just do what you have to do to keep Lotti's and your employees safe." Em will never forgive me if she loses her mom's business.

"It's not the money I'm worried about." He sighs. "I've gotta handle this. If you've got any breaking news or plans, please let me know. I should be back at Em's within the hour."

"If the media find her place, take her to my home. I'll let security know you might be heading their way."

"Yeah, okay."

"I'll talk to you later after practice. I'm really sorry, man."

"Hey, Nightly. This isn't your fault. You didn't do this on purpose. We'll figure it out and go from there."

"Thanks, B." I hang up before his sympathy has me feeling even crappier than I already do. It is my fault, despite what he and Austin say. I didn't cause Em's pain in the past, but this—last night and today—is on me.

I barely make it through the doors before I'm stopped by Rocco, our GM; Coach Alan; and Charlie, head of PR. This can't be good. It's not like I thought they wouldn't find out. I just hadn't taken the time to reach out to them directly.

"Hey, Nightly," Rocco extends his hand, "we'd like to talk for a minute before you head to practice."

I glance at Coach as if he'd override the GM. "Do I need to get my team on the phone?"

"I've already got calls in to Austin and Angela," Charlie advises. "They should be on the line by the time we make it to the conference room. Summer is in there now opening up the conference call."

Fuck. Do I need to call Em? I don't want to leave her in the dark, but I also don't want to drag her into discussions dredging up her past before a plan is in place.

My phone rings as I near the conference room. I answer right away. "Willa, hold on just a sec." I lower my phone, pressing it to my leg, and advise Rocco, Coach, and Charlie, "This is my sister. She's with Emmeline. I need to be sure she's okay. Give me a sec, please."

Coach pats my shoulder. "Sure. Join us when you're done." By the softness around his eyes, I can tell he's not pissed at me. I don't know what I'll do if the Dragons take a stance against my girl, but I'm pretty sure it won't be in their favor.

I slip into an empty office and close the door. "Sorry about that. What's up?"

"Do you remember my friend Timothy? He's a producer at the *Today Show*."

"Vaguely." I lean against the desk, pinching my nose. "I'm a little worried why you're bringing this up now."

"Emmeline and I were talking. If you're okay with it, the *Today Show* is interested in interviewing the two of you—"

"What?!" My first response is to say *no*, but she… "Wait, you said you and Em were talking. Does that mean she's open to the idea?"

"She is." There's caution in Willa's voice.

"What kind of story are they interested in? I've no interest in Em getting blasted or shamed for something that was *done to her* when she was sixteen." I start to pace. It feels too good to be true—too simple of a solution.

"They want to give her a chance to tell her story and the impact of it coming to light so many years later. They're also interested in learning whether you knew of her... *attack* before the story broke yesterday."

"And Em is okay with this?" I'll talk to her before making any decision, but I need to clarify again before I mention this to the Dragons' management.

"Yes, I confirmed before calling you."

"I'm about to walk into a meeting with my GM, Coach, and head of PR. Can you send me his contact information? I'll probably have Austin coordinate if we decide to do it, but I need to talk to Em before agreeing to anything."

"I figured as much. I'll send the details. Then we can discuss after your game."

"Okay. Thanks for sticking with Em." I hated the idea of her being alone.

"I wouldn't be anywhere else. I know what she means to you and what you mean to her."

"I love her, Willa. She's the *one,* and if I have to give up my job to protect her, I'll do it. In a heartbeat." A calm seeps through my bloodstream at that admission. *I would give it all up for her.* It's a weight lifted.

"Let's hope it doesn't come to that."

CHAPTER 31

EMMELINE

BASED ON HOW MY NIGHT ENDED AND MY morning started, I never would've bargained on attending tonight's game. I'm worn out, even though I've done nothing but couch surf and try not to panic over being in public after all the news reports I tried not to read. I was only marginally successful at either of those.

They think I'm a gold digger and Nightly didn't know about my sexual assault. The truth is, it's none of his business. I have every right to keep that trauma to myself. However, I did share those details because I wanted to let him in past the barriers I've fortified over the years. I didn't want to keep him at arm's length like most men I've encountered.

Nightly is different, in every way. I hope tonight he can see that and begin to forgive me for this morning. I was scared and took it out on him—our relationship. I love him, and I need to prove it to him.

We're all three decked out in Colorado Dragons gear from head to toe. I have my hair in a high ponytail sporting a green, white, and black pompom. Willa went with pigtails, same accoutrements. Bennett is sporting a Dragons Beanie. We all have on Nightly's jerseys, though mine is actually one of his he insisted I have. And to round out the ensemble, we have Dragon's scarves, black jeans, and green high tops on our feet. I don't know where Willa managed to snag those on such short notice, but I'm thankful she did.

Then there's my sign. It's folded in half, sitting on the floor between my legs until he takes the ice. I'm so nervous, I may pass out. My heart beating this fast can't be good.

"You look like you need a beer." Willa leans in to speak to me and Bennett, who's on my other side. I wanted them to sit together, but they insisted I sit in the middle. I'll admit I feel safer not on the edge chancing a not very nice stranger sitting next to me.

"I think I need a morphine drip," I joke. It was a bad one though. It brings back memories of that night. I had morphine the first twenty-four hours after my attack. I was alone, terrified of my surroundings, and in so much pain from a jawline fracture and how brutally they invaded me. I'm not sure if the hospital only gave it to me for the pain or to shut me up—probably a bit of both.

While I'm lost in thought, the opposing team's introduction begins as they fill their bench and the startling line up is announced. It's not until the house lights dim and the Dragons' intro music blasts from the speakers that we're on our feet cheering with everyone else. What an amazing feeling it must be to have fans flock to your games to cheer you on, celebrate every win and commiserate losses. Imagine if every job had fans; going to work might be a lot more entertaining.

As the smoke fills the ice and the laser show continues, the Dragons' starters are announced. I'm screaming by the time I hear Nightly's name, and he takes the ice, skating with the other starters to the blueline. For a second, he scans across our section, and then his head whips back, locking on me.

"The sign!" Willa screams, helping me hold it up.

"What if he can't read it?" I should have made it bigger.

"He has excellent eyesight. How else do you think he keeps track of the million-miles-an-hour puck?" She laughs.

"He sees it." Bennett's hand rests on my hip. "He sees you, Puddin'."

Nightly says something to the guy next to him and skates forward, then all of them head toward the glass in front of our section. Nightly scans the sign, his gloved hand pressed to the glass. Then his eyes are back on me, all smolder and grins.

"God, he's beautiful." I want to touch him, hug him, say the words he so deserves to hear: *I'm sorry. Please forgive me. I love you.*

Instead, I mouth the three words that matter most: *I love you.*

"Don't make me puke, Em. He is my brother." Willa raises the sign over our heads, pointing at it to be sure it's seen by everyone.

"Damn, we're on the jumbotron." Bennett nudges me.

But my eyes are all for Nightly, who lays his hand over his heart and says, *I love you, Em* and then points at me. This time, I nearly do faint.

"Steady, Em." Bennett grips me tighter. "The world is watching. Let them see your love—your strength."

An older gentleman from the bench—I assume his coach—is yelling at Nightly and his teammates, who are dancing behind him making goo-goo eyes and saying *I love you*, to get their asses center ice or be benched. Nightly gives me one more look before heading for the man—his coach. They have a quick conversation that has his coach looking my way and nodding, agreeing to whatever Nightly's saying.

Satisfied, Nightly makes his way to back to his team's blueline with the other starters, and the National Anthem begins to play. His eyes stay on me the whole time. I've never been so visible. When it's over, I get a single nod before he skates to the center for the face-off to start the game.

I barely remember sitting or hiding behind the sign until I catch my breath, swiping at a lone tear. He saw me. He saw his sign. The world didn't end by stepping out in public and being vulnerable in a big way, letting them know he's mine and I'm his. We're not just dating. We're in love, and I'm not afraid of letting the world know—not anymore.

Willa hands me her phone. "You're already making news."

I watch the screen as the whole thing plays out on the jumbotron. I can't hear what's being said, but the caption reads, *Love on the Ice.*

That's a headline I don't mind.

"How did you find that so fast?" I hand her phone back.

"I have an alert set if anything with either of your names shows up on the internet."

"Well, I don't want to see any of the bad ones, please."

She squeezes my hand and pockets her phone. "These are all good, Em. You're inspiring."

NIGHTLY

After my meeting with management and another quick call with Austin, practice was pretty much a bust. We were a disaster. It wasn't only me, though. It felt like the team was feeding off my energy.

Most of the starters were at the charity event last night, and those who weren't were pretty quickly read in on what was going on with my girl. Not a single one made a snide, disrespectful comment at practice, not even the rookie. They were all, "Sorry," and "Who do I need to beat up?" and "Tell your woman we have her back." That one nearly did me in, had me on the brink of tears. All I wanted was to be home with her in my arms, consoling her, telling her I'd make it right in whatever way I could.

My team deserved better than I gave them at practice, but once I saw her in The Lair, in the seats I'd reserved for her, Bennett, and Willa, the added pressure lifted, and I could take a full, cleansing breath. Then she beamed at me, sandwiched between my family and hers, holding up a sign that declared her love for me. That damn sign is getting framed and hung over our bed. A permanent reminder I won the jackpot with her.

The starting face-off was a joke. The Philadelphia Hawks' center decided to make a crack about Em. He thought it would throw me off my game. It didn't.

I stole the puck, took it to their net and scored with an assist from Alec. Their center got slammed by Kells, my left wing, who heard the comment. The poor guy had a hard time staying off the boards whenever we passed him. He's a bully. His whole team is. It's a pleasure to steal the puck every time they try for a goal.

It'll be even more enjoyable to serve them a shut-out game.

CHAPTER 32

EMMELINE

IT'S THE SECOND PERIOD, AND WE'RE SCREAMING for Storm and his linemen to make a goal. They're toying with the Hawks, making them eat crow for every nasty hit or word exchanged. They have a reputation, and it didn't mislead. They're a foul bunch. But the Dragons are kicking their asses down one end of the ice to the other. It doesn't seem fair. It's like the Hawks are second string compared to the entirety of the Colorado Dragons.

My man is racking up the points. I couldn't be prouder.

"Em." Bennett nudges me, motioning to the gentleman crouched next to him.

"Hi, Ms. Weston. I don't know if you remember me—"

"Brooks, right?" He's the Dragons' family relations person or something like that.

"Yes, ma'am." He seems pleased I remember him. "Mr. McNight wanted me to check on you and see if there's anything you need."

"Anything?" I mean, I am hungry.

"Yes, anything. Food. Drinks..."

"I'd love a Coke and some loaded nachos." I feel like I haven't eaten all day, when in fact, it's basically all I've done.

Brooks makes a note on his phone and looks at Bennett and Willa. "And you, Mr. Sterling?"

"Same but add a soft pretzel and mustard." He leans back so Brooks can see Willa.

"And you, Ms. McNight?"

"A Sprite and two hot dogs with mustard, ketchup, and sweet relish." She beams.

"Excellent. I'll have those delivered shortly. But before I do, I wanted to let you know the Colorado Dragons' GM, Rocco Gallo, has invited you to his suite for the remainder of the game, if you're interested."

"Oh, I... uh..." I look to Bennett and then Willa questioningly.

"It's up to you, Em." Bennett pats my hand, leaving it there for reassurance.

"I'm game either way," Willa states.

"Please tell Mr. Gallo, though I really appreciate his offer, we're going to stay here. I'd hate for Nightly to look and find us missing and make him worry." I lean closer. "Plus, I really like being close to the action."

Brooks laughs. "I don't blame you. Mr. Gallo thought you might say as much, so he's extended the offer to after the game. Mr. McNight would join you as well."

"Okay. I guess it would be rude to turn down Nightly's boss."

Bennett and Willa agree.

"I'll be back to get you when the game ends." He hands me his card. "Call me if you need anything in the meantime." He stands. "Your food and drinks will be delivered shortly."

"Thank you, Brooks."

"My pleasure, Ms. Weston, Ms. McNight, Mr. Sterling, enjoy the game." With that, he descends back to the bowels of The Lair.

"Wow," Willa comments.

"What do you think that's about?" I eye Bennett before checking out the game and find Nightly on the bench looking at me. He gives me a wink before turning his focus back to the game.

"I think you and Nightly made national headlines. Mr. Gallo wants to meet his star player's significant other and be sure you won't embarrass the franchise." Bennett's brow furrows on a shrug.

"Brutally honest, as always." I nudge him.

"Sorry."

"Don't be."

"If it eases your worries any, his daughter was attacked a few years ago." Willa squeezes my hand.

"Was she—" I swallow the lump in my throat.

"Unfortunately, yes. She's doing fine. She works in the office. But Rocco will have nothing but sympathy for you. I wouldn't worry about him. He'll be on your side," she assures.

"As much as I hate that for her, it does make me feel better knowing he has some idea what it's like to be close to a survivor—the impact it can have." At least I hope he does. As a man, I imagine it's hard to relate to the helplessness a woman can feel.

NIGHTLY

The final goal is a slapshot delivered by Kells with an assist from Alec and myself. When the final horn blows announcing the end of the game, we win 11-0. I couldn't be happier for the shutout.

Philly didn't deserve to win with the bad sportsmanship they showed tonight, continually ragging on Em, thinking eventually it would rattle me. What it did was piss off my team, making it personal for all of them, and they came at the Hawks in full force. As for me, it was upsetting, only it made me more determined to end the game as soon as possible so I could get to my heart. She showed up for me—for us—in a big way.

Coach let me skip the press conference afterwards. We decided speaking to the press tonight would not be the best move. Inevitably, a question about Em would have come up. I prefer to speak about Em with her present and not bog down the win with personal talk that has nothing to do with hockey. So, once I'm showered, I'm on my way to the GM's box to meet my girl, Bennett, and Willa.

I round the corner to find Em holding up the wall, with Bennett and Willa standing protectively in front of her. She spots me over Willa's shoulder. Her hand flies to her mouth as her face crumbles. Bennett and Willa's heads whip my direction and relax when they realize it's me.

"Thank God." Bennett approaches with my girls in tow. "Great game." He pats my arm.

I pass with a quick, "Thanks."

I press a kiss to Willa's cheek. "Thanks for coming.' Then I wrap my other girl in my arms. "Baby, please don't cry."

"I-I'm so sorry," Em sobs.

I find Brooks standing a few feet away, and before I can even ask, he offers, "There's an empty suite here, if you want some privacy." He unlocks the door and ushers us in. "I'll tell Mr. Gallo you'll be a few more minutes."

After picking up Em, I take a seat in the corner, giving us as much privacy as the suite allows. "It's okay, Em. Here." I hand her a few tissues I grabbed on my way to the couch.

She dabs at her eyes, worrying about her makeup. "I can't meet your boss looking like a raccoon."

I kiss her cheek and wipe a few stray tears. "You're beautiful.

Besides, Rocco will understand. He knows it's been a stressful few days." I frown. "Has it only been a day?"

"Yeah, nearly twenty-four hours."

"Dang." I scrub my face. "I know we have lots to discuss, but the most imperative before you meet Rocco Gallo is the interview. Are you sure you want to do it?"

She nods. "I'm sure. I have to own my past, not cower away from it. I'm tired of giving people power over my own story. If we want different, we have to write the narrative. Direct the ship where we want it to go."

"Wise words." I cup the back of her head and lean in. "I need a kiss, Em. Tell me you forgive me for getting us into this mess."

"You didn't do anything wrong—"

"If it wasn't for me—"

"I'd be alone and have no idea what true love feels like. I won't ever regret meeting you—falling for you. You've opened my eyes to what my life could be like, and I can't unsee it. Don't regret me, Night. I don't regret you."

"Never. I'll never regret falling for you, beautiful. Not in a million years."

"Good. It's settled then." She presses her mouth to mine and kisses me torturously slowly. "It's you and me against the world."

"God help anyone who stands against us."

"Exactly."

"I love you, Em."

"Love you right back, Carter."

Another quick kiss before a knock at the door. "Time's up," I whisper. "Time to meet the man."

She laughs. "I've already met the man, and he stole my heart."

I love this woman. "You stole mine right out of my chest."

She extracts herself from my lap. "You're taking me to your place when this is over."

I clarify, "I'm taking you home to *our* place as soon as we meet Mr. Gallo."

"Deal." She lifts her hand, offering me her pinky.

I wrap mine around hers. "Deal."

I'll happily pinky-swear with this woman for the rest of my days.

"Let's get this over with."

I'll fight with her. I'll fight *for* her. I'll love her, on her, and for her. I'll protect her heart and her body—not that she needs my help in that regard. She's a warrior off the ice. I'm a warrior on. Together we're formidable, undeniable, unbeatable.

CHAPTER 33

EMMELINE

MY HAND SECURED IN NIGHTLY'S, HE LEADS US into Mr. Gallo's suite. Bennett and Willa are close behind, with Brooks closing the door behind us. Introductions are quick and courteous. Mr. Gallo's a large man, probably played sports in college or maybe pro. I'll have to ask Nightly later.

Gently, Mr. Gallo asks for the room, and his remaining guests say their good nights and leave without any fanfare. His eyes land on our joined hands before meeting mine.

"I wanted a chance to meet you, Ms. Weston. I'm truly sorry your private history is being unearthed because of your relationship with Nightly and The Dragons." He squeezes Night's arm in reassurance. "My daughter was assaulted a few years ago. Maggie is doing fine now, but still there are times the memories cloud her eyes, dampen her spirit." He clears his throat, notably struck by the impact of what she went through—continues to go through. It's obvious he loves his daughter very much.

Before I consider it too familiar, I grip his hand hanging at his side. "It's a process. I hear she works for the Dragons. I imagine having you close is a comfort to her."

He smiles. "Yes, she works in marketing. She loves it and is quite talented. I admit, I like having her under my roof. I wasn't blessed with sons, but my daughters are my pride and joy, and having one of them involved in my legacy means the world."

It shows. "I'd like to meet her sometime, if she's interested."

"Oh, she's interested. She called me last night when the story broke. Said I needed to meet you and let you and Nightly know we support you in whatever way you need." He extends his hands, taking mine and Nightly's. His hold is firm. "I mean that. Whatever you need, the Dragons are here for you both." He squeezes again. "And on a more personal level, I'm here for you even if there comes a time we part ways. You've earned my respect and loyalty, Nightly. Whatever you need."

Nightly moves first, embracing the man who is obviously more than a boss. "I appreciate it, Rocco. The next few days will be tough. I don't want to let the team down, but I also need to be there for Emmeline." He pulls back and secures me by his side with a firm grip on my waist and hip.

"Speaking of, if you're serious about the *Today Show* interview, we've got a plane lined up to take you there in the morning. It'll be a private, prerecorded interview with a small crew. No audience and not live." He motions to a gentleman in the corner, who hands him an envelope. Rocco in turn hands it to me. "All your travel details are enclosed. Nightly will obviously accompany you. We've arranged a nice hotel stay for you and dinner. Then return flight the next day."

"I... wow. Thank you." I'm flustered and wasn't prepared for this level of support. I expected scrutiny and vague acknowledgment of my situation, not kind words, hugs, and a dinner.

"Listen, I can only imagine how difficult this is for you, having to relive what those men did to you. Go do the interview, set the record straight, but don't feel obligated to share more of yourself than you're comfortable with. It's your story, your life, and no one gets to tell you how you should feel about it." His voice gets stronger and firmer as each word passes his lips. I imagine him saying the same thing to his daughter.

"Maggie is lucky to have you, Mr. Gallo. Thank you for supporting Nightly and me. You could have taken a cold stance and made it all so much more… challenging. But knowing Nightly's team is behind him—and me—means the world." I move forward, and he encircles me in bear hug like I've never experienced. Maybe this is what it's like to have a father.

I swipe at my eyes as I step back. "Thank you for everything. It was a pleasure to meet you."

"It's my pleasure, Ms. Weston." Mr. Gallo shakes our hands. "Austin and a few lawyers, mine and yours, are traveling with you tomorrow. It's on us. You don't need to pay for a damn thing. I just want to be sure everything stays on the up and up, and you're granted the respect and dignity you deserve." His eyes land on me.

This man is going to make me full-on sob if he doesn't stop being so nice. All I can do is nod on a soft "Thank you" to keep from breaking.

We say our good nights, and before I know it, we're in Nightly's truck heading to his place. Bennett and Willa are following in B's car. They're going to stay in the pool house to give us the alone time we need.

"That went far better than I thought," I admit.

"Agreed." Nightly squeezes my leg. "I mean, I've known Rocco to be a good and fair man, but I was worried he'd put the franchise's needs over ours."

"I can't believe they're flying us to New York. I thought it would be a remote video conference interview, if anything."

"Are you okay with this?" His furrowed brow is reassuring.

He'll support me even if I change my mind. "I'm more than okay. We get a night in New York." I can't hide my excitement. "I know the interview will be rough, but topping it off with a night in the city that never sleeps sounds wonderful."

He kisses my hand, setting it on his thigh. "Then it'll be wonderful. I'll make sure of it."

NIGHTLY

I can't get my woman alone fast enough. After saying g'night to Willa and Bennett, I walk Em backward to my room, my hands firmly on her hips, guiding her. "I need you naked and holding up your sign for me."

"Oh," she gasps, and the heat traveling up her neck to her cheeks is so fucking satisfying. I hope I never stop surprising her with how much I want her.

"You were sexy as fuck staking your claim over me, in front of my team, coaches, boss, and the whole damn world. Let that image go viral. Let every soul on earth know I'm yours and you're mine."

"Night." Her hands press to my chest, their warmth spreading, urging me on.

I lean into her touch. "I love you so much, Em." I practically fall into our kiss, holding her to me as I take the few steps to the bare wall next our bathroom door. I break our kiss, stepping back. "Get naked."

I lock the bedroom door and pick up the sign where it dropped a few feet away. I lay it on the bed as I start to strip, watching as she does the same, growing harder with every inch of skin she reveals. "That's it, beautiful, show me what's mine."

"Night." She shudders, her shoulders rise, her fists clench, and her nipples harden. She fights to stop herself from wrapping her arms around her chest. She's fucking stunning, and still she's modest. Or is it uncertainty?

The last of my clothes land on the floor, and I stalk toward her, setting a box on the dresser beside her. "Is your need to hide your body because you're modest or because you don't fully comprehend how much I crave and love every inch of you?"

When her palms land on my stomach, my eyes close, and my head falls back. "Fuck, you're so warm." She slides her arms around my waist, moving into me, nuzzling close. I wrap her in my arms, sinking my fingers in her hair, tilting her head to meet my gaze. "You didn't answer me."

One shoulder rises as she stares her truth into me. "I'm used to hiding my body around men. It's safer to not be sexualized, particularly in the military. It's a hard habit to break." She squeezes my ass and rubs her belly along my cock caught between us. "Plus, you're sexier than ten grown men combined. It's hard to compete with the body of a professional athlete."

On a growl, I pick her up, holding her thighs until she wraps them around me. I press her into the wall, thrusting my cock into her awaiting heat. "Fuck." My forehead falls to hers. "You make me crazy and impatient."

I pull out slowly and buck forward, filling her till my balls are the only part of me not planted deep inside her. "I wanted to taste you first, make you come on my tongue. But you go all shy and tender on me," I pull out and shove back in, "and I just need to fuck you till you feel the extent of my need for you."

"Yes," she moans, driving me senseless with her sounds, her body, her scent.

I pound and pound until her head falls back and she screams, "Carter!" as she comes on my cock.

"You squeeze me so fucking good, baby." I pinch her nipples and suck her tongue, ravaging every part of her I can touch, grinding and fucking her into her next orgasm until she's panting and mindlessly saying my name on repeat.

Still deep inside her, I grab the box and lay her over the edge of the bed, her legs tight around me, I slowly push them open and pin her knees to the bed, spreading her wide for my viewing. "Look at you taking my cock so fucking good, Em." Her juices coat me, the sight turning me on impossibly more.

Opening the box, I pull out the small pink vibrating butt plug, holding it up so she can see it. "I want to put this inside you."

Her heavy-lidded eyes blink at me as she moans her consent, "Yes."

"Good girl." I press my mouth to hers, just a swipe of my tongue as I turn the vibrator on and rub it through her wet folds, pressing it against her opening, where I'm filling her in slow strokes.

"Oh, fuck," she gasps, shaking and surging into me.

"You like that?" I press it against her again, nearly slipping it inside her with my cock.

"I'm gonna co—" she screams as she comes and gushes around me.

"Fuck." I pull out despite her protest and slip the vibrating plug inside her just enough to hit her G-spot.

"Oh, God! Oh!" she cries. "Yes, right there!" Moisture shoots out of her pussy, drenching me, the bed, the floor. I keep rubbing it and bend down to lick and suck her clit. A few more seconds and she's squirting again.

"Fuck, Em. I'll never get enough of you coming all over me."

Slowly, with her knees bent and her pussy and ass in the air, I work the now silent vibrator into her ass. She wiggles and squirms, trying to take it deeper. "Patience, Em. I don't want to hurt you."

"It doesn't hurt." She catches my eyes and smiles. The love shining there has me pushing a little harder until it sinks past the ring of muscles. If it wasn't bulbous on the end, she would have sucked the whole thing inside.

"You doing okay?"

"Yes," she pants, a little in awe, I think. "Will you turn it on?"

"In a minute." I reach past her to the box again and close my fist around the last item. "There's something I need to do first."

I release her legs, pull her farther up the bed, and loom over her, running my hands over her arms to her hands and back up, watching her nipples harden. I take one and then the other between my teeth, nipping and sucking deeply.

"Oh!" She rubs against my still hard cock between us. "I need you inside me."

"Me too." My hips circle, grinding against her, spreading her juices, making a mess of her and me. This next time, when she comes, I'm coming with her. I lean back on my haunches, knees wide, her legs over mine. I hold her left hand over my heart and slide a diamond ring onto her finger.

As her eyes widen in surprise, I thrust home, filling her completely, reaching around to turn on the butt plug. The sensation hits her instantly, and she bucks, the vibration hitting my cock from inside.

"Fuck!" I fight, holding my release at bay.

"What?" She holds up her hand. As I start to slowly fuck her, she grips my thighs and moves with me. "Are you going to ask me?" she manages through her mewls of pleasure.

"Do you need the words?" I'm totally going to ask her. I'm just building up to it.

"Yes, please, Carter."

I lean over, changing our positions, covering her body with mine, only holding my weight on my bent arms near her head. "I love you, Em. It might seem soon, but it'll never be soon enough for me."

I thrust, grinding her clit with each motion, dying to pound my love into her. "Marry me, beautiful. Move in with me. Have babies with me."

Her beautiful cunt squeezes me in response to the baby remark. *Fuck!* I quicken my thrusts with the thought of filling her full of babies. I suck her nipples hard and deep, and pound, every thrust filling the room with the sounds of our wet joining. "I love you, Em. Say *yes*. Be mine."

"Yes!" she pants, "Yes!" She grips my ass and squeezes. "Yes!" She comes, soaking me, milking me until I'm filling her with my release.

I devour her mouth, consuming her cries and moans in a kiss that shatters and puts me back together in a form that's only made for her, only she fits.

Later, cleaned up and resting in our bed, she smiles at the ring on her finger. "It's beautiful, Carter."

I kiss her head and tip her chin. "You're beautiful."

"No, you are," she teases.

"I'll only accept that from you in the privacy of our bed, but call me beautiful in front of the guys, and I'll never hear the end of it."

She smiles deviously. "And what if I do?"

"I'll have to punish you." The edge to my voice is no joke. She'd love my form of punishment.

She squirms in my arms. "Like spanking?"

I laugh and swat her ass. "You'd enjoy that, wouldn't you?"

She tips her head. "Maybe."

I'm reminded of her coming all over my cock as I spanked her clit. "You'd definitely enjoy it."

We're quiet for a moment before she sits up, holding the sheet across her chest. "What about Bennett?"

"Hmm, I hadn't thought about it, but if you want me to spank him—"

She swats my stomach. "No, silly." Her face softens, and her eyes catch mine. "If I move in here—"

"When—"

She rolls her eyes. "*When* I move in here. What happens to him?"

"He moves with you, if he wants. He has a pick of a guest room or rooms, or he can have the pool house, but he might have to share with Willa when she's in town."

Em plops back down, laying her head in the crook of my arm as she gets comfortable on her back. "I don't think she'll mind."

"I don't either." And that's the honest truth. We haven't discussed what they have going on. I figure they'll share when ready.

She links her hand with mine. "It means a lot, you know. You accepting him in my life. Few would do that."

"You won't get the chance to find out, because you're mine, and you agreed to marry me." I roll on top of her, making space between her thighs.

Her smile is everything. "I did. Though I'm not sure that's a proposal we can share."

I tease her nipple hard and press my growing erection against her pussy, already needing to surge home. "Well, I guess I'll just have to do it again while not buried inside this sweet pussy of mine."

"Yours? Then your cock is mine."

I kiss her chin and catch her golden gaze. "I thought you already established that when you showed a sign to the entire world that you love my *package*." I wiggle my eyebrows and relish her blush.

"I can't deny it," she grinds against me and sighs, "I do love your cock."

"Good 'cause he loves you too."

"I think I need to show him how much." She flips me to my back.

I choke on my laugh at how easily she did it. "It's hot when you find your brave." I kiss her nose. "Come here, baby." I grip her hips and rub her wet pussy along my length. "Ride your cock, show it who's boss."

She rises to her knees and sinks down my hard length, taking every inch.

"Fuck, Em."

"I love your dirty mouth. Later I want to ride your face."

"Yes, fuck, please." I throw my head back and lose myself in the sight of her riding me vigorously. I knead her tits and tweak her nipples. "Take what you need."

Her eyes land on mine, and she smiles sweetly. It steals my breath. "You're exactly what I need, Carter."

I pray she always feels that way. "Same, Em. Same."

THE END

EPILOGUE

EMMELINE

MY PALMS ARE SWEATY, AND I'M FIGHTING THE urge to puke all over the seat in front of me. Nightly tightens his grip on my hand. "It'll be fine, Em. It's a private interview. No audience. You have the right to not answer any question."

He thumbs over his shoulder to the team at the back of the plane: his agent; his personal PR person; and two lawyers, his personal one and the team's. "They'll keep the interview on track. No matter what, we walk if we don't like the direction it's heading."

I nod, hearing what he's saying, but my body is screaming at me to just turn the plane around now. I don't know the first thing about talking to a reporter. I'm not eloquent. I'm not trained in these tactics. This is out of my wheelhouse. "What if I make it worse?"

"Timothy, Willa's friend, said they want to help us turn the narrative. I don't believe they'd try to trick us into making fools of ourselves." He tips my chin, catching my gaze. "I promise, Em, I won't let anything bad happen on the air or off. I'm your shield. Let me protect you from this. Give me your fears. Concentrate on your truth."

"Concentrate on my truth," I repeat out loud then to myself.

My truth. "I can do that." I let out a punch of air and deep-breathe until I'm calmer. I can do this.

I can't do this.

"Breathe, Em." Nightly squeezes my hand as a tech checks the lighting around us. I wish we were sitting on a couch so I could feel his warmth pressed against my side. I hate being afraid. Give me a mission, a destination, a goal, and I'm there, my Marine hat on, pristine in my uniform, my shield against whatever happens.

But this, sitting in a plush chair next to Nightly in an identical chair, surrounded by lights, mics, cameras and the ominous chair facing us, makes me want to puke. I almost wish we were sitting at a table, something to hide behind, something to lean on, something to crawl under when the questions assuredly get too hard to answer.

"Emmeline." Timothy, Willa's producer friend, squats in front of me. "I can see the panic in your eyes. I swear Hoda will make the interview as smooth as possible. She's a pro, but more important, she's a wonderful human. She doesn't work for us fulltime anymore. She called wanting this interview if we were lucky enough to have you and Nightly say yes. If you need to take a break, ask, and we'll turn the cameras off and regroup."

I nod, unable to find my words without tears joining them.

"Thanks, man." Nightly pats Timothy's shoulder. "Could we get some water maybe?"

"Of course." He stands. "I'll be right back."

"What do you need, beautiful?" Nightly's eyes are solely focused on me.

"For this to be over."

His smile is indulgent, patient. "Why are we here?"

I frown. He knows why we're here. His brows punch up, waiting. "To set the record straight?" Right?

His head dips as he moves closer. "To give a voice to survivors who can't speak for themselves—"

"Or have the opportunity to share their story. To stop being a victim. To stop the shaming." I *know* why I'm here. I forgot for a moment.

"That's right." He kisses my hand, sitting on the edge of his chair, angled toward me. "Why are you here, Em?"

"To speak for those who can't."

He lets out a punch of air and nods. "You've got this. *We've* got this."

Timothy returns, setting *Today Show* mugs full of ice water on end tables beside our chairs. His gaze flashes between Nightly and me. "You look better. Hoda is on her way. I'll be just over there," he points to a chair beside one of the cameras, where Nightly's agent, PR person, and lawyers are waiting. "Look my way and tap the side of the chair, and I'll stop the interview—or just ask for a break."

"Thank you," I breathe out, feeling calmer knowing there's an out if I need it. Not that Nightly hadn't said the same thing over and over again. It's good to know the show feels the same—or at least Timothy is on the same page.

"I've got you. Willa would have my balls if I let anything happen to you two." He winks before stepping back to speak to the crew.

I turn to face Nightly. "You sure you want to do this? You'll forever be associated with the girl who was—"

"*Is* a badass?" he interrupts my negative thoughts bubbling to the surface. "I'm all in, Em. I think we need to work in Raven's Hope too. Get them some free publicity. Let it be known they have a crisis line and can help anyone who needs it."

"God, I hope Joey is ready for that."

"He will be. I've got Austin working on getting him the funds and support he needs."

"What?!" I nearly come out of my chair but stop when I see Hoda making her way toward us.

"Joey and Raven's Hope will be fine." He squeezes my hand as Hoda nears. "Breathe, baby. We've got this."

I smile at him, knowing no matter what happens, he won't let me fall, or if I do, he'll be the first one there to help me get back on my feet. "I love you," I whisper. Tears that never seem too far off threaten to make an appearance before we even get started.

He flashes to me, heat simmering in his eyes. "Love you, woman. So fucking much."

Timothy hurries over, a silly smile lighting up his face. "Um, just a reminder. Your mics are live."

Nightly laughs.

I groan, "Oh, God," and fight the desire to sink into my chair, hiding my face.

"Everyone in the control room is swooning over you two. No worries. I just wanted to mention that before—" he eyes Nightly, "this one takes it to a whole other level."

He would too. My man has a talented mouth, in words and action.

A few moments later, the cameras are rolling and Hoda's smiling face is solely focused on us. "Firstly, it looks like congratulations are in order..." Her eyes flash to my ring, and a smile breaks across my face. *This* I can talk about. A calm seeps through me as Nightly starts to speak of our love being inevitable.

I can do this. I squeeze his hand and join the conversation.

NIGHTLY

"That was perfect." Hoda stands, coming over to hug my woman. "You did such a good job." She shakes my hand. "I think you'll be proud when you watch this back."

"Thank you taking such care…" Overwhelmed with emotions, Em's been fighting tears nearly the entire interview, and now they fall freely.

"Thank *you* for letting me share in telling your story. The world needs more positive role models of what tragedy turned to triumph looks like."

Em laughs, her embarrassment written all over her lovely face.

"I keep telling you you're a badass." I pull her into my side. "So proud of you."

She buries her face in my chest for a second before I wrap her in my arms. "I couldn't have done this without you."

I want to correct her, saying she wouldn't have had to do this if it wasn't for me. But it's a can of worms we can't put a lid on now. She's accepted me and the certain level of fame my job brings us. We move forward from here as a team. "I wouldn't have wanted to be anywhere else." I kiss her forehead. "Ready to get out of here?"

"Yes," she softly replies.

Hand in hand, we thank Hoda, Timothy and the rest of the crew and make our way outside to our awaiting driver. My agent, PR people, and lawyers left as soon as the interview was over, needing to get the ball rolling on getting the word out.

Now it's just us, ready to take on New York in whatever way Em feels up to doing. "Hotel or food first?"

"Hotel. I want to wash this makeup off my face and get comfortable." She fastens her seatbelt, noting the crowd around Rockefeller Center.

Thankful we're not known well enough to be bothered or recognized, I take her hand and settle in beside her. "I'm onboard with that." Not all that crazy about the makeup on my face either. "Hotel, please," I tell the driver.

"Fuck, Em." I grip her hair, guiding her greedy mouth along my hard-as-steel cock. "Not gonna last if you keep sucking me like that." Fuck. Me.

She moans, sucking harder, doubling down, sending shockwaves of pleasure to my balls. She dropped to her knees as soon as I closed the suite door behind us. I was lost in the view for a few seconds before I realized what my naughty woman had in mind.

"Jesus," I growl, pumping my hips, and groan when I hit the back of her throat, causing her to gag and squeeze my tip. I back off only to shove back in, seeking the sensation again and again. "This fucking mouth."

I lose myself in her enthusiasm, pumping a handful of times before pulling her off my cock with a pop. "I'm not coming down your throat, Em," I pant, fighting the urge to do just that.

"What—"

I haul her to her feet, taking in the state of her wrecked makeup before capturing her swollen mouth in a voracious kiss, feeding her my tongue in deep strokes and sucking retreats. Walking her backwards, I divest us of our clothes, fumbling our way to the bedroom, then to the ensuite bathroom.

Turning her toward the counter, I grip her hips and squeeze. "Spread your legs. Show me my pussy."

"God," she moans and gasps as I eat her out from behind, licking her ass-to-clit and back before shoving my tongue in her drenched pussy. "What the hell?" she gasps, tensing.

I pull away, meeting her eyes in the mirror. "What?"

She points to her face, grumbling, "I'm hideous."

I growl and stand, bracketing her back. I tip her chin so she meets my eyes full-on. "Don't say that shit about yourself. You're fucking perfect."

Her whole body shakes in a laugh. "You're delusional, Night. Have you seen my face?"

"I'm looking at it."

"Then what the fuck?"

I capture her bottom lip, sucking before licking her taste into a heated kiss. "You're wrecked over sucking my cock, Em. I couldn't want you more."

She sighs, releasing the tension riding her for the last few seconds. "Really?"

I grind my cock against her ass, dipping till the tip hits her core. "Fuck." My forehead lands on her shoulder. *How does she feel this good, and I'm barely inside her?* I meet her gaze in the mirror. "Does it feel like I don't mean it?"

"No," she mewls as I push inside her sweet heat.

I forget what we were talking about as I grip her hips and watch myself sink in further. "This fucking pussy is going to be the death of me." I pull out and surge home. "So fucking tight and wet." Reaching around, I grip her breast and cup her mound, rubbing her clit, the tips of my fingers grazing my cock as I stroke in and out, ratcheting my arousal. "I'm gonna come so fucking hard, Em."

"Yes!" She squeezes her other breast, twisting her nipple as she braces against the counter with her other arm.

I regret I don't have more hands to simultaneously grip her hips, tease her breasts, play with her clit *and* asshole while also having another cock to fuck her ass at the same time as her pussy. If I could do all of that, we'd never leave the bedroom or the house, for that matter. I'd remain buried inside her sweet body from here to eternity, coming and coming, pumping her full of my seed till she begs me to stop and then begs me to do it all again.

"Carter!" She arches into me, swiveling her hips, using both hands on the vanity as leverage.

"Yes, fuck, just like that." I pump harder, deeper, faster, never letting up on her breast or clit. When her legs start to tremble, I slap her clit, holding her tight, doing it again before rubbing in circles.

"Fuck!" She gushes, losing the ability to hold herself up and folding forward over the counter.

I grip her hips, loving the change of angle and the sight of my soaked cock pistoning in and out of her. The best sight ever. Better than the image of her swallowing my cock down her throat. But the vision of both set me off. "Need you to come, baby. I'm gonna fill you up."

And fuck if she doesn't. "God. Carter," she moans, shaking.

I shove through her walls, squeezing the everloving fuck out of my cock, sucking and pushing at the same time, stealing my breath, my sight as I pump my release into her. "So good. So fucking good, Em," I pant over her back as I fall over her, trying to fill my lungs with air and the sweet scent of her as my cock continues to twitch, making her gasp when her pussy flutters.

Later, much later, I finish my feast by eating her as dessert after room service and a much-needed nap. The stress of the last few days washes away in the shower we share, along with the knowledge that whatever comes, we're a team. We're in this together. As she rides me into oblivion, the vision of my future wife—not too distant though—fills my head with the dream of fucking her full of babies, enough for our own hockey team.

I tweak her nipples and swipe her clit into two orgasms as I growl my approval across her heated skin and come like a rocket.

All night, we fuck, make love, and devour. It's heaven. It's our future we're creating together. The warrior and her hockey god—her words, not mine. A dream made in heaven, written in the stars, and made true by believing we deserve more than one-night stands and surface-level connections.

She nuzzles into my neck, swinging her leg over my half-hard cock. "I just need a few minutes of sleep, then I need you to do that again."

I chuckle and squeeze her ass. "It'll be my honor, Em."

She kisses my jaw. "It's my honor, Night. Love you."

"Love you." I press my lips to her forehead. "Forever, baby."

"And ever," she trails off, finally succumbing to her exhaustion.

She's under my skin, in my heart, and in my bed. She's my other half, and I can't wait to make her my wife and start on those babies.

Thank you for reading Nightly and Emmeline's love story. Would you like to see what they're up to years later? Then scan the QR code below to access bonus content for them as well as further reading recommendations.

If you have any questions or concerns, please feel free to reach out to me: dana@dmckdavis.com

ADDITIONAL BOOKS BY
D.M. DAVIS

UNTIL YOU SERIES
Book .5 - Until You Fall
Book 1 - Until You Set Me Free
Book 2 - Until You Are Mine
Book 3 - Until You Say I Do
Book 3.5 - Until You Trilogy (Books 1-3)
Book 4 – Until You Believe
Book 5 – Until You Forgive
Book 6 – Until You Save Me

FINDING GRACE SERIES
Book 1 - The Road to Redemption

BLACK OPS MMA SERIES
Book 1 - NO MERCY
Book 2 - ROWDY
Book 3 - CAPTAIN
Book 4 - COWBOY
Book 4.5 - A Black Ops Christmas
Book 5 - MUSTANG

ASHFORD FAMILY SERIES
WILD Duet
Book 1 - WILDFLOWER
Book 2- WILDFIRE

STANDALONES
Warm Me Softly
Doctor Heartbreak
Vegas Storm
FACEOFF

dmckdavis.com

AUTHOR'S NOTE

If you've been following me for a while, you know I've struggled these past few years with my mom's illness and subsequent passing. FACEOFF is my first *new* release in a couple of years. It was wonderful to finally get back to writing and breaking in those old muscles that hemmed and hawed a bit but finally got back in working order.

I'm thankful to Nightly and his Em for opening themselves up so I could tell their deeply heartfelt love story. I love those two. Gah, and Bennett, he stole my heart. I wasn't sure what to make of his and Em's friendship at first, but they generously let me in and showed me the way. Thank you, Nightly, for being open and comfortable in his own skin enough to support his woman and her bestie in the way they needed and deserved. Respect.

Thank you to my husband and my kids for their endless support and understanding as I found my footing again and passion for telling the stories I hear in my head.

Thank you to my author friends, Divas, and my PA Ashley Blank for your support and sticking with me. You feed my soul and lift me up. I am eternally grateful for you.

Thank you to my editors, Tamara and Krista, for *still* being my editors despite my long dry spell. They make my words shine and my stories coherent.

Thank you for readers, both new and seasoned, for reading. I couldn't do this without you. If you haven't read my other series, I hope you pick one up and fall in love with a whole new set of characters. There's much more to come.

Keep reading. I'll keep writing.

I'm blessed to be on this journey. Thank you for taking it with me.
XOXO, Dana

ABOUT THE AUTHOR

D.M. Davis is a Contemporary and New Adult Romance Author.

She is a Texas native, wife, and mother. Her background is Project Management, technical writing, and application development. D.M. has been a lifelong reader and wrote poetry in her early life, but has found her true passion in writing about love and the intricate relationships between men and women.

She writes of broken hearts and second chances, of dreamers looking for more than they have and daring to reach for it.

D.M. believes it is never too late to make a change in your own life, to become the person you always wanted to be, but were afraid you were not worth the effort.

You are worth it. Take a chance on you. You never know what's possible if you don't try. Believe in yourself as you believe in others, and see what life has to offer.

Please visit her website, dmckdavis.com, for more details, and keep in touch by signing up for her newsletter, and joining her on Facebook, Reader Group, Instagram, X, and Tiktok.

STALK ME

Visit www.dmckdavis.com for more details about my books.

Keep in touch by signing up for my Newsletter.

Connect on social media:

Facebook: www.facebook.com/dmdavisauthor

Instagram: www.instagram.com/dmdavisauthor

X: twitter.com/dmdavisauthor

Reader's Group: www.facebook.com/groups/dmdavisreadergroup

TikTok: www.tiktok.com/@dmdavisauthor

Follow me:

BookBub: www.bookbub.com/authors/d-m-davis

Goodreads: www.goodreads.com/dmckdavis

dm DAVIS

SEXY WITH HEART ROMANCE

CONTEMPORARY & NEW ADULT ROMANCE AUTHOR

Printed in Dunstable, United Kingdom

82086133R00160